GODDESS
SON OF MEDUSA

A NOVELLA

Todd Crawshaw

CrowsnestPublishing.com

Visit: www.toddcrawshaw.com

ISBN: 979-8-9882757-0-1

Book illustration & design by author

CrowsnestPublishing.com

Printed in the United States of America

ALSO BY TODD CRAWSHAW

Amulet

The Center's Edge Revisisted

Portrait of a Rainbow as a Young Man

God, Sex & Psychosis

heretofore

Light-Years in the Dark

Exploits of the Satyr

GODDESS

Cast of Characters

ASTER: Medusa's offspring

MURPHY: Private investigator

ELDOR: Aster's birth father

ARION: Aster's step brother

MORRIS: Eldor's employee

NATE: Bartender and Aster's housemate

ADRIANA: Murphy's friend and attorney

PERSEUS: Mercenary and assassin

ANDROMEDA: Perseus' wife

MANNY: Waiter at The Goddess

LARISA: Nate's girlfriend

TRITON: Eldor's eldest son, Aster's step-brother

BELUS: Aster's step-brother #3

GODDESS

"Underestimate me. that'll be fun."

— unknown origin

GODDESS

PROLOGUE

My mother was a monster. Her beauty turned men into stone, if you believe the myth. In truth, she was born into slavery, owned by a cruel woman who considered herself a goddess. As a joke, she bestowed the title of priestess onto my mother whose duties were to clean the house, a sizable mansion, and attend to her mistress' needs. My mother's incredible beauty turned the heads of men who desired her to themselves. She was sought after by many men. Her mistress, jealous of this attention, deprived my mother of pleasure. She was to remain chaste and celibate for life. As a domestic prisoner, fearing the wrath of her owner, she shunned the advances of men. That is, until she was raped by a sea captain – her mistress' uncle.

Blamed for the rape, for seducing him, my mother was set free as her punishment. Her hair was shorn, her scalp shaved. She was cursed by her mistress and banished from the mansion, forced to enter the outside world completely naked. Adding insult to injury, she discovered later she was pregnant with me. I don't blame her for becoming a monster. With one look she would turn men into stone. Not a metaphor. She did. Because of this power, she was beheaded. Upon her decapitation, did twin sons – a winged horse and boar – fly out of her body? Was her head then placed on a shield to destroy enemies with her deadly gaze during battles? The latter two *are* metaphors. Untruths. I was her only true son.

Let me begin again. Mother did have stunning hair. This is true. It grew back in sweeping black coils that resembled writhing snakes. Men became petrified by her beauty. I witnessed this myself when I grew old enough to know better. When she became angry at me for some misdeed, I avoided eye contact. Men who dated her, especially those who were racist or approached her with bravado or arrogance,

1

learned this devastating lesson, not to look, too late.

Did I love my mother? I did. She was pretty, also frightening, not always a monster. She had tended bar for a living. It is fallacy that simply looking at my mother turned the living into stone.

She would warn first, "Be careful how you look at me."

It would always be men who didn't heed her warning. Growing up, I witnessed these stoned men who could not believe their fate. Whenever it happened at home, my task was to guide these catatonic zombies out the front door. When she was working the bar pouring drinks, everyone presumed the paralysis was alcohol-related. Often I would be seated at a table, sipping on a soft drink, and she would look my way to give me a sly wink.

Her demise was caused by men who spread rumors she was evil and a misandrist. Not true. She had male friends who were good. Who trusted her. And women who were attracted to her strength and ability to ward off the toxic masculinity. Survivors of sexual assaults even wore tattoos resembling my mother with wild snakes for hair. Her beheading escalated her fame, turning her into a legend.

The cause of my mother's death, I will explain. But first allow me to indulge in the telling of my story.

I am a freak of nature. I had no idea what that meant until my mother was beheaded. She had always protected me from the truth. I was – what is the current term? – homeschooled. Mother taught me all I know. She did not prepare me for the cruelty of this world. How people would judge me as being abnormal – born an hermaphrodite. That I was both male and female seemed an important discovery, once I understood the difference. As an only child, isolated from kids my age, I never questioned my sexuality, a term that went beyond my years of understanding. Mother dressed me as a boy and had always called me her son.

Her murder happened around the time of my puberty. Imagine my shock when told my mother was dead. I was then abducted into social services as an orphan and placed into the foster care system. The monthly bleeding meant I was dying too. The examinations only made my pain worse, to realize I was a medical curiosity. I became suicidal when my body rebelled against me and grew breasts. I was mortified by these changes. I was teased and tormented by this uncertainty about whether I was a boy or a girl. I am a mix of several diversities. As one who is both black and white, I have been called many names, but no word or label could define me.

Mother told me I was a demigod, given my birth from the rape of a powerful man I never knew or cared to know. Powers would come to me. And they have. I can read minds. It is one of my unique gifts. Not like Tiresias, the blind prophet, gifted with clairvoyance, who had the ability to see into the future. He too had been turned into a woman after being attacked by mating snakes, transformed from male to female. That is not my fate. I am not blind. I have vision. Also, I inherited my mother's ravishing looks and raven hair cascading from my head like writhing snakes.

1

Aster was tending bar at The Goddess on a busy Friday night when a new customer sat on a bar stool in front of her while she was preparing a martini.

"The apple doesn't fall far from the tree."

She heard the words and gave the man an askance look as she shook the canister of gin and ice.

"And by that, you mean what?"

"I know about your mother."

"Doubtful. You're a private investigator."

The man tilted his head, "Lucky guess."

"It wasn't a guess. Your thoughts scream loud and clear to me. Tell me what you really want."

"A scotch on the rocks. When you get a chance."

"You want to solve my mother's murder."

"That too. My name is Mitch—"

"Murphy. You're wasting your time. And mine."

Aster walked away to deliver the martini at the end of the bar. Murphy admired her stride, dressed as she was in a sleeveless faux snakeskin top and a black leather skirt.

When she returned, she saw the business card in the detective's hand extended toward her. She plucked the card from his fingers and deposited it in the tip jar. "Scotch on the rocks, you said?"

"A Naked Grouse, if you happen to have it."

"We do." Aster reached to find the bottle behind her on the wall and twisted off the cork as she turned back. She poured a generous helping into a glass over ice. She slid the cocktail toward him and assessed this man. She determined he was in his mid-thirties. He had straight longish hair that touched his shoulders. He was aware of his good looks which explained his confident and playful grin that, no doubt, could charm women.

"I like your hair," he told her. "It is pretty wild, and beautiful, same as your mother's?"

Aster folded her arms. "I already know who killed her."

Murphy lifted his drink, taking a sip of scotch before setting it down to reach into his coat. He pulled out a small notepad and pen, prepared to write. "Who?"

Aster's steely-grey irises bore into Murphy. He averted his eyes from what felt like staring into the sun. Blinded for a lost moment, he blinked, disoriented as he regained his focus – alarmed to discover he was naked. He nearly fell off the barstool.

Aster had a thin smile. "You're not worth the trouble. I won't turn you into stone. You can relax."

Customers were vying for her attention but she was unmoving, staring directly at him.

Murphy realized he was not naked. "How did you—"

"Carl Jung. Does that name sound familiar?"

Murphy rubbed his eyes, regathering his thoughts, and wrote down the name in his little book.

Aster gave a laugh. "You're not as smart as you look. I can see that you are searching your memory. The psychiatrist? *Jung.*"

"Oh." Murphy smiled, chagrined. "Right. The guy who wrote about the collective unconscious?"

"And the dark side of masculinity. The fear of snakes. Feminine mystique and power." She turned to glance at a customer raising a hand and his voice to get her attention. "Collective *man* killed my mother. Does it really matter who it was, specifically?"

Murphy opened his mouth to reply but felt his thoughts calcify, left speechless.

Aster told him, "I need to get back to work."

2

Eldor watched Aster with great interest. He held a Lager beer, seated in a booth with two of his shipmates. His spies had informed him, years ago, he had sired a boy. What other lies had he been told? As he drank, he mused. This supposed son he traveled to meet turned out to be a daughter. An intriguing young woman as gorgeous as her mother, who had presumedly been transformed into a monster.

"What do you plan to do with her now, Captain?"

"Shut up, Morris," said Eldor, "I'm thinking."

"This son of yours is awfully pretty," joked Arion.

Eldor glared at his quartermaster, whose smile froze, deflecting a confrontation by picking up his beer.

With his eyes aimed at Arion, Eldor said, "If looks could *kill*. Have you heard that expression?"

Arion nodded.

"Her mother had that ability. If you believe all the stories."

"Are you saying your daughter might have that power?"

"Don't be an idiot, Morris. It's a fucking myth!"

"Deadly snakes for hair. Get real," said Arion. "These fables. They're all bullshit. What was she called again?"

"Medusa." Eldor scanned the barroom to survey the strange assortment of people. A man was racking billiards wearing a kilt. The woman beside him wore leather pants. She playfully tapped him on the ass with her cue stick as he leaned over to break the balls.

"What the fuck is this place? Who are these people?"

"Your daughter does have amazing hair. Oh, shit," said Morris. She's looking straight at us. She's coming over here."

"She's made us." Arion lowered the brim of his cap.

"We're not invisible," said Eldor. "She knows nothing."

Aster crossed her arms as she looked down at the three men, studying each for a moment. She said to Eldor. "You're him. My father. Why are you here?"

Eldor gave a puzzled frown. "Have we met?"

"You *raped* my mother."

Eldor smiled, lifted his beer. "Welcome to the world."

Morris snorted a laugh then flinched as Aster turned her eyes on him and glared. "You *are* an idiot."

"I didn't *say* anything," said Morris.

"You didn't have to. And you, *Arion*. You only *wish*. Maybe I'll *fuck* with you again."

Eldor said, "What is she talking about?"

"Nothing." Arion clenched his jaw.

Aster started to leave then turned back. "You disrespected one of my waiters. Manny said you were rude, calling him names."

Morris smirked, "That's rich. His name is *Manny?*"

"Emmanuel. Did you call him a queer?"

"But he *is*," said Arion. "Isn't he?"

"We're all queer," said Aster. "Gender neutral. And of the lot of us here tonight, you three are the queerist of them all."

"Listen, sister—"

Eldor stopped Arion from speaking with a raised hand. He was nonchalant. "What the hell is this place?"

"Mine."

"Do you have a name, daughter of mine?"

"Aster." She scoffed at him, "You're a captain of what?"

"A ship. She is called the Poseidon. I rule the sea."

"I knew you'd be arrogant and full of *lies*. Enjoy your beers then get the hell out of here. And don't ever come near me again."

"Or?" Eldor grinned.

"You'll regret it."

3

Aster returned to her station behind the bar and saw Murphy still seated there, watching her as he nursed his scotch.

"What was that ruckus all about?"

"None of your business," said Aster.

"It *is* my business." Murphy grinned, glancing back at the three men in the booth. "An unsavory bunch by the looks of them."

Aster was gone when he turned back. She had moved down the bar to remove empty glasses left by departing customers.

The other bartender, a muscular man wearing a black t-shirt and satin vest, approached him, pointing to his empty glass.

"Another round?"

"I'm thinking I might want something else," said Murphy.

"What can I get you?"

Murphy pointed toward Aster. "Her."

"She's unavailable."

"Not for sale?" Murphy joked and extended his hand across the bartop. "Name's Mitch. What's yours?"

"Nate." He made a fist for Murphy to bump.

It was past midnight and the bar crowd had thinned to only a few patrons left seated at the bar.

"Have you been working here long?"

Nate was wiping the bartop with a towel. "Long enough. Did you want another drink or not? We close in an hour."

"Sure. I'll have another Naked Grouse, if you please."

As Nate poured the scotch, he said to Murphy, "You're not her type if you were thinking of making a play for her."

"What *is* my type?" Murphy's smile wasn't returned.

"Aster doesn't date. I know this for a fact because we share a house. Our relationship is platonic. My girlfriend lives with us too."

Murphy was processing this information as he watched Aster return and reach into the tip jar to retrieve his business card.

"I changed my mind," she said. "Are you any good?"

"Good at what?"

"Your profession, Sherlock."

"Specifically, what did you have in mind?"

"Investigate those three men. Find out what you can."

Murphy sipped his scotch. "Give me a clue. How do you know them? Have they harassed or threatened you in any—"

The one with the large beard, not the smaller one, the big guy, he is my birth father. We finally met for the first time."

"Wait. Was he your mother's lover?"

"No! He *raped* her. She didn't know the man. She was enslaved, then banished after becoming impregnated with me – from *that* man. You should know this since you're keen on investigating her murder. How much is this going to cost me?"

"Depends on how deep the rabbit hole turns out to be. I charge ninety dollars an hour. The search to find your mother's murderer is pro-bono. No charge."

"I know what pro-bono means. Do you want an advance?"

"That's not necessary. I trust you."

"Don't be a fool," said Aster. "Trust no one. Nate, take out five hundred dollars from the cash register."

Nate handed her the money. She placed it on the bartop.

"Write me a receipt for the advance in that little notebook and we will have ourselves a legal arrangement. Your drinks tonight are on the house. Pro-bono. Do we have agreement?"

Aster reached across the bar. Murphy shook her hand.

"I expect results."

4

A week later a woman dressed in a business suit with a stylish cut to her short blond hair came into The Goddess and stood at the bar, waiting for Aster to notice her.

When she did, Aster approached the woman with a cautious bit of concern, reading her mind. "You're Murphy's attorney."

"How could you possibly know that?" She held out a business card. "My name is Adriana. You must be Aster."

Aster took the card. "Why is Murphy in a hospital?"

Adriana's strictly-business composure dissolved. "What's going on here? How did you—"

"I read your thoughts. It's my little trick. Reading minds."

Later, Aster and Adriana were standing at the foot of Mitch Murphy's hospital bed. His eyes were shut and the skin around both sockets was swollen and bruised. Adriana's thoughts were a jumble of concerns that were unreadable.

"How bad is he?"

"He's not in a coma," said Adriana. "He's just sedated. There's the visible contusions to his face, broken ribs, and a mild concussion. He'll survive."

"How did this happen?"

"He won't tell me. He said he wanted to speak with you first. He told me where to find you."

Aster sighed, "This is all my fault. I hired him to—"

"Mitch knows the risks in his line of work."

Murphy opened his eyes and smiled, wincing from pain. "You did come. I wasn't sure you would."

"Of course I came," said Aster. "I'm not a monster."

"No, of course not."

Aster said, "I can't read your thoughts. What happened?"

Murphy tried to shift his body upright in the bed, but winced from pain and remained lying flat on his back. "Do you want to hear the good news or the bad news first?"

"There's good news?"

"You were lucky to be born a girl."

"Why?"

"Your father intended to abduct you onto his ship."

"You mean, shanghai me? Why?"

"Your father is a drug trafficker. Let's call him a pirate. He was under the impression he had a son. He was going to take possession. But bringing a female to work on his vessel would be considered bad luck and weaken his authority with the men."

Adriana said, "Did her father do this to you, Mitch?"

"He had help. He doesn't care for snoops."

"God damn him! We need to have them all arrested."

Murphy rolled his head on the pillow. "Adriana, I don't see that ending well." He smiled at Aster. "You escaped being abducted into a pharmaceutical drug cartel. That's the good news."

"And the bad news?"

"I discovered who killed your mother. He wasn't hard to find since he brags about his exploits. He's a mercenary fortune-hunter with a hero complex. He receives help from powerful patrons."

Aster repeated, "And the bad news?"

"He knows you exist. Because you are your mother's offspring, someone believes you're a monster who should be terminated. This assassin, who calls himself Perseus, has been hired to kill you."

"I'm not a monster! Who wants me dead?"

"That I haven't discovered yet."

5

Nate was helping Aster clean up after closing the bar. He was observing her fastidiousness – more like obsessive compulsiveness – arranging and straightening the liquor bottles on the mirrored wall. He was reluctant to comment on her behavior but did.

"Are you scared?"

Aster froze, turned, and snapped at him, "Of course I am!" She stepped away from the liquor bottles and leaned against the bartop. "Sorry, Nate. I'm sorry. I don't know what I'm doing."

Nate came over to embrace Aster, holding her head in his hands against his chest. He was not used to her being this vulnerable. She was always the one in control. He felt her body shaking and stroked her back to soothe her.

"We will find a way to protect you—"

Aster pushed away and wiped her eyes. "Hiring private security, bodyguards? I can't have people following me around and watching my every move. This is insane."

"I know."

"Someone wants me dead. Why? I've done nothing wrong."

Nate averted his eyes.

"What?"

"You have embarrassed and angered a few customers."

"Who deserved what they got."

"Aster, I'm on your side. But the mind games, these tricks you play, sometimes go too far. But nothing that warrants—"

"*Murder*. God, Nate, what I am supposed to do?"

Someone was tapping on the glass panel of the front door.

Aster screamed, "Can't you see we're closed!"

The tapping continued, getting louder.

"Stay here." Nate left the bar to take a closer look. "It's that guy you hired. The detective."

"It's okay. Let him in," said Aster.

Murphy came in, shaking off the rain. He removed his hat with a nod to Nate and approached Aster, who was behind the bar.

"How have you been?"

"Afraid for my life," said Aster. "How are you?"

"Better."

"You still look like hell."

"It hurts when I laugh." Murphy smiled, held his chest, and sat at the bar. "You don't like my yellow and purple complection?"

"Have you come up with any bright ideas?"

"About your situation?"

"Yes, my situation. Did you want a drink?"

"Desperate for one. Please."

"Naked Grouse?"

"You know me already."

"Don't push your luck." Aster reached for the bottle and took two glasses, filled both with ice, and poured the liquor.

"Ah, you're going to join me?"

"I need this. Talk to me."

Murphy lifted his glass, tasted the liquor. "I have a plan."

Aster scoffed. "You have a plan. Okay, what is it?"

"You won't like it."

"Tell me."

Nate was hovering behind Murphy. "Tell her."

He gulped more scotch. "My plan is to get to know this Perseus fellow and convince him not to kill you. And I'm going to propose a counter offer."

"How much is this going to cost me?"

"It depends on how much your life is worth."

6

Perseus was basking in the sun, lounging naked beside a pool bordered by large rocks that overlooked the ocean. Several men and women were there with him. When he saw someone approaching, he shielded his eyes from the sun's glare with a hand and said, "Ah, it's you again. What in Hades' name are you wearing?"

Murphy looked at his shorts, tropical shirt, and sandals.

"Strip down if you want to talk to me."

Murphy glanced at the women and men, each in their birthday suits, smiling back. He was hesitant to undress.

"What's wrong with your face?"

As Murphy unbuttoned his shirt, he smiled and said, "I ran into a confrontation."

Perseus laughed. "It looks to me like you lost. Your chest is quite colorful too. You could use a tan."

Murphy unbuttoned his shorts, dropping them to the ground, kicking off his sandals too.

Perseus pointed. "Look how small you are!"

This produced laughter from his gaggle of friends.

Murphy felt himself shrinking even smaller, embarrassed by the remark. "I get bigger." He shrugged and sat on a boulder.

"I should hope so," said Perseus. "But size, rumor has it, does not really matter. Or does it, girls?"

Murphy heard the women tittering.

"I am just messing with you, Mitch. You have some red in your face now to offset the yellow and purple. "So speak to me. Bare your soul. Why are you here?"

"To bargain with you. I have a request to make."

Perseus expressed interest, rubbing himself with a glance at the woman beside him. "Do you need someone killed?"

"Yes, and no. Do you know a ship captain named Eldor?"

"Hell yes! He abducted my wife and chained her to a rock!"

Murphy had struck a nerve. "Why did he chain—"

"Because that man is *sick*." Perseus gathered his composure. "This 'captain' saw her beauty and forced himself upon her. He thinks he is a god who takes what he wants. He is the most ungodly person I know." Perseus laughed. "But my bride-to-be fought back valiantly, resisting his forced hand upon her head, biting and hurting him. Appalled and angered, Eldor punished her by having his men chain her naked to a rock for the high tide to drown her or a sea creature to devour her."

Perseus gestured to the woman lying by his side. "This here is Andromeda. My wife. The woman I rescued." He leaned toward her and they exchanged a passionate kiss on the lips.

"Is it true you killed a sea creature?"

Perseus grinned. "With a special sword. I have powerful friends. That is what I do, Mitch. Destroy monsters."

"This Eldor is who I had the confrontation with."

Perseus scowled, then chuckled. "I guess you want that bastard killed too?"

Murphy felt his confidence growing. "If you hate this man so much, why haven't you?"

Agitated by the question, Perseus stood, turning away to stare at the sea. "Eldor manufactures drugs and is in league with Mexican cartels. He poisons people for profit. He *is* a monster. Do you think it is easy being a hero?"

"Eldor also raped a woman who you murdered."

Perseus turned back, curious. "Who?"

"The woman who was described as having snakes for hair."

"Are you joking?"

"Is it true?"

"*Is it true?*" he echoed cynically. "I still have her head in a sack. Did you want to take a look for yourself?"

Murphy flinched from Perseus' wicked grin.

"That woman *was* a monster. Why do you care?"

"Because her daughter is not."

"Is not what?"

"A monster. Aster is a good person."

Perseus reached behind a boulder. He took hold of a sword and raised it for Murphy to observe. "So that is why you are here?"

"I'm in love with her. The way you love Andromeda."

Perseus stared thoughtfully at the sharp blade, then lowered the sword, touching its sharp tip into the surface of the swimming pool. The calm water rippled, creating rings. "You will find it amusing to discover who it was that hired me."

"To kill Aster? Who?"

"I believe you mentioned a bargain?"

7

Arion awoke from a nightmare bathed in sweat, shamed, and embarrassed, which turned to anger. He kept reliving the nightmare. Was it real or had he imagined it? He rolled over in his bed, clutching the sheets, wanting rest but remaining restless. What had happened in that bar? From what he could recall, he had a couple of beers. Had his drinks been spiked? His memory of the incident that night was mostly a blank except for flashes of public nudity. Never would he have done what he did unless—

The bosun's whistle fully woke him. The signal was an order for all hands on deck. Something was amiss. He rubbed his eyes, then raked fingers through his hair, cursing this woman, this step-sister. She did something to him. Somehow she had mind-fucked him. He was certain of it now. She was evil.

Arion dressed quickly. He was the quartermaster and needed to be informed. His father was a tyrannical taskmaster. A man who was unpredictable. He viciously killed all rivals without forethought. To be on Eldor's shit list was like being issued a death sentence.

The view outside the porthole of his stateroom showed fog and a hint of sunlight. He braced himself for the day, looking at himself in the mirror. He saw the eerie resemblance, the face of the man who raped his mother. He had grown a beard because his father told him it would make him appear more manly. Compared to his father, he had a slight stature. His beard was slight too. He felt he could never measure up to his imposing father, who had him in servitude. He was not the only one on the ship who was the product of a rape. He had step-brothers. Because of his genetic shortcomings, Arion knew he should appreciate his elevated rank over the others on this enormous vessel – a luxury yacht, essentially.

Eldor was standing on the helicopter pad with the entire crew assembling around him. His face radiated a pent-up fury. When he saw Arion, he signaled for him to come near. Eldor held a sheet of paper which he thrust overhead with the sea breeze slapping it in his clutched fist.

"I received an anonymous letter. Someone explain to me what this means!" He brought the sheet in front of his face to read: "Your position of power no longer intimidates us! It is time to step down! Your rule has come to an end! Relinquish control or your stockpile of laundered wealth will disappear with a few keystrokes! Warning, the contract to have your daughter decapitated is on hold!"

Eldor shook the sheet of paper. "Tell me why I received this! Who knows about this threat of a coup? How does this involve my daughter? Is she being held hostage? Is this a ransom note?"

He turned his head toward Arion who shook his head to deny any knowledge of the letter. The crew muttered their innocence too. The captain roared, "Whoever sent this will never get a god-damned cent from me! She is not my responsibility. I just met the woman. But when I discover who is behind this threat to my power, heads *will* roll. Back to your stations!"

As the crew scurried away, Eldor grabbed Arion by the arm and pulled him toward the helicopter.

"Where are we going?"

"You will know when you need to know. Get in."

Arion saw that Eldor's henchmen were already inside.

8

Murphy was at an outdoor cafe with Adriana having lunch, sharing a bottle of wine.

"As your attorney, I advise you to drop this case."

Reaching for the bottle, Murphy removed it from the bucket of ice and poured them both more wine. "I'm afraid I am already way in over my head."

"Exactly my point," said Adriana.

"Meaning, I can't easily extract myself. I'm in too deep, to use another lame expression."

"You're risking your life for this woman. Why?"

"I think I'm in love." Murphy smiled and raised his glass.

Adriana lifted her glass too, tapping his in a mock toast. "Well, congratulations. I'll be sure to attend your funeral. Did you wish to be cremated or buried in a box?"

"Come on, Adri. Be happy for me. She's beautiful. She's—"

"Dangerous." She stuck a fork into her salad.

"I suppose that is part of her charm. She fascinates me."

Adriana looked across the table at Murphy and sighed, taking a bite of the shrimp. "Tarantulas fascinate me. So do deadly poisonous snakes fascinate me. But I don't want them near me."

Murphy shook his head, bit into his Reuben sandwich. "Hum, this is really good. Listen, I appreciate your concern but, like I said, I'm head over heels for her. I have to stop using clichés. Anyway, you know what I mean."

"Does she feel the same way toward you?"

Murphy laughed. "No. Not at all. But she will. Eventually."

"After you save her life? She will be indebted and fall madly in love with her guardian and protector. Is that the plan?"

"Can you stop being so cynical. Why don't you like her?"

"She can read minds. Did you know that?"

Murphy recalled the moment he actually thought he was naked on a barstool. "Yes. Among other things."

"Tell me. I'm curious to know."

"Nothing." Murphy took another bite from his sandwich, then washed it down with some wine. "What?"

"You know something you're not telling me. Could she be as dangerous as her mother?"

Aster doesn't have snakes for hair that can turn men into stone. And is that story even true?"

"She has hair that *resembles* snakes."

"Stunningly beautiful hair." Murphy grinned.

Adriana did not return the smile. "And this psychopath you met with, on her behalf, for her sake. Again, his name?"

"Perseus. Though I'm not convinced he is a psychopath."

"Mitch, he's a mercenary. He kills people."

"Only those who he considers to be monsters."

"You said you convinced this assassin to hold off on killing her. How? What was the bargain you made with this devil?"

"That is between him and me."

"I'm your attorney, Mitch. Also a friend. I need to know."

"I made a promise not to tell anyone else. That was part of the deal we made."

"I hope and pray you know what you are doing."

"So do I, Adriana, believe me. So do I."

9

Aster watched as Nate chopped up vegetables in preparation for a stir-fry dinner. She enjoyed the sound that the wok made when it sizzled and smoked. She envied her housemate's culinary abilities, which she lacked, for lack of interest. Her mother never got around to teaching her how to cook.

"Mother died before she could warn me about being a girl, and the dangers of becoming a woman. To answer your question."

Nate stopped chopping to look over at Aster's smile.

"I can hear what you're thinking."

"I know," said Nate. "It spooks me more than a little."

Aster shook her head. "No, I lost interest in wanting to be a boy. Especially when I learned how mean boys could be. I didn't want to be one anymore. But puberty was pure hell."

"It wasn't a picnic for me either," said Nate as he used a knife to move slices of chicken into the wok.

"I like when it sizzles," said Aster. "Did you want me to pour you some wine?"

"Sure. Thanks."

"Nate, I'm just saying you got off easy being born normal."

He laughed. "You think I am normal?"

"You never had to experience getting a period after thinking you were a boy born with a pre-pubescent penis."

"Okay, that's true."

"And, yes, it still hurts. I like that I am a woman, but the first time I was called a *girl* – and not in a nice way – I cried. I would cry myself to sleep almost every night."

Nate gently stirred the wok with the spatula. "I'm sorry."

"Don't be. It's the culture we live in. I tried my best to adjust to what I was and to fit in, attending school for the first time with other kids. But the gossip about my abnormality was non-stop. I was never placed in a foster home, to be adopted. No surprise. Along with the teasing, I learned male intimidation was also a *thing*. 'Shut up, bitch' became a common refrain."

Nate poured a splash of the red wine into the wok. "Aster, I've never known you as one to be silenced."

"I had to learn to speak up for myself. A boy once said to me, 'You should have your tongue cut out.' He was serious."

"When was this?"

"After a school debate. It was when I first realized I could read minds. I saw my opponent's thoughts and turned them against him. I had him so confused and tongue-tied, he stormed off the stage in tears, embarrassed to be soundly defeated by a girl."

"Men have fragile egos. We need to feel empowered."

"So do women. Anyway, I'm glad we're having this candid talk. What else did you want to know, but afraid to ask?"

"I'm not afraid of you, Aster."

She smiled and drank some wine. "Maybe you should be."

"No. I trust you."

"Good. I trust you too."

"Do you trust Manny and the others to work the bar tonight without all hell breaking loose?"

"Yes," said Aster. "But the answer is *no* to your other question. My mother was never an unsightly hag. That myth evolved because powerful women scare men. Things that frighten people are thought to be ugly. Like spiders and snakes. Because men were frightened by her power, she was depicted as a hideous monster. That's why she was beheaded. And murdered while she slept!"

Nate shook his head in sad disgust, pouring the stir-fried dish into a bowl. "Are you relieved by what Murphy told you?"

"My reprieve from being murdered didn't sound like a certainty.

I have no idea what he's up to. It's all very clandestine. He says it has to be. Should I believe and trust him, Nate?"

"He is smitten with you, I know that. It's pretty obvious the way he looks at you. I notice these things."

"He sees me as some ideal. Which I am not."

"No one is perfect. I hope you're still hungry."

"Isn't Larisa joining us?"

"She's working a late shift at the hospital. So, no. I'll save her some of this deliciousness for later. Dinner tonight is for us."

"How much does Larisa know about me?"

"Your condition?"

"Yes, Nate. That I'm intersex."

"Larisa doesn't know."

"She must have suspicions. I never date and—"

"She doesn't know. This is our secret."

10

Arion tried to contain his nervousness. He had no idea what country they were in when the helicopter landed. Had they crossed borders? The location was remote, in a mountainous region with no visible access by four-wheeled vehicles. He saw no signs of roads or trails traversing the slopes. He hoped the roar of the rotor blades was loud enough to hide the rumblings in his acid-filled stomach. When he saw another helicopter on the plateau, he tasted more fear and swallowed.

"What's going on?"

"Shut up," said Eldor. "I'll do the talking."

As they landed, scattering dust, they all remained inside until the air settled. Once they had a clear view of the other aircraft, Eldor's henchmen exited, armed with semi-automatic weapons. Armed men debarked from the other helicopter. Eldor nudged Arion, signaling it was his turn to go. His father stepped outside last, protected by his row of guards on the ready.

Each small battalion approached the other and stopped.

Eldor directed his words at the man standing behind his flank of armed guards. "Triton, I gave you life. How dare you challenge me. Shall we kill each other now, or talk?"

Triton was as imposing as Eldor. He held a trident-shaped object over his shoulder. He brushed a strand of his long thick hair off his shoulder and struck his chest. "You, Father, are the aggressor. You threatened me!"

Eldor stroked his beard. "Then explain this message!"

Arion watched as his father thrust the sheet of paper in the air. "You no longer fear my power? Relinquish control or my money will disappear! And what the hell is this warning?" He brought the letter in front of his eyes. "A contract on hold to decapitate my daughter? What do you call this – if not a threat!"

"Not from me," said Triton. "I received almost the same letter. The only difference, she was called my sister."

"Liar!"

Triton handed the letter to one of his men who handed it to one of Eldor's men. Arion stepped forward to retrieve it and handed it to his father.

Eldor scrutinized the letter and looked up. "I know you've been encroaching on my territory and stealing money from me. Do you take me for a fool?"

Triton grinned and joked, "Mi casa es *su* casa. No?"

Eldor was not amused. "Don't challenge me. Who created these letters, if they didn't come from you?"

"My house is clean. Yours might be dirty. Look inside."

Arion saw his father was on the verge of unleashing his rage. This would not end well if he did.

"Father?"

Eldor turned his eyes on Arion. "You'd better have something relevant to say."

"Someone outside our family could be responsible for sending these letters, these veiled threats. And what if this woman is killed? Should we even care?"

"My sentiments too," said Triton. "I was curious to inspect this offspring from Medusa, a woman you raped, Father, who had deadly snakes for hair."

"She did *not* have snakes for hair when I seduced her."

"Nor does your daughter, my sister, at present." Triton removed the trident-shaped weapon off his shoulder and struck the shaft on the ground. "I made an incognito visit to her establishment. This bar is a disturbing place. She somehow knew who I was, even though I revealed nothing about myself. The experience I had was upsetting.

From the encounter, I determined she was evil."

"So did I," said Arion.

Eldor frowned. "Why is she evil? I've heard nothing from either of you that justifies her death. I found her to be lovely, though brash, and as beautiful as her mother."

"Who turned into a hideous monster," added Triton.

Eldor rebutted sharply. "And what if this daughter of mine does not? I've sired many sons, a few disposable, but only one daughter. It will infuriate me if I find that she had been murdered as the result of an unjustified contract kill."

Eldor turned abruptly and spoke over his shoulder.

"Triton, discover who is responsible for these threats, if not you. I trust you to find the source. Be the loyal son I rewarded, inheriting the spoils from our trade. Who I entrusted to divide them according to my instructions! We will meet again to continue this conversation when you have answers for me."

11

Murphy was seated inside The Goddess' dimly-lit bar at noon. The place was sparsely populated at the lunch hour since no food was served, only alcohol and snacks. Drinking a beer and munching on complementary nuts from a bowl placed on the bartop, he stared at Aster moving about, servicing the few customers.

She returned to stand in front of Murphy.

"I can feel your eyes watching me and I hear your thoughts as if on a non-stop loop. Why should I have dinner with you? What is my incentive?"

"Food. Wine."

"I don't go on dates."

"Call it a business meeting. You do eat. You must."

Aster studied his smile. "I'm not what you think I am."

"No? You are not a beautiful woman?"

"Listen, Murphy—"

"Call me Mitch. You owe me that much for saving your life."

"You only postponed the inevitable, *Mitch*."

"I'm feeling more confident about your longevity than you."

Aster folded her arms. "How did you convince this assassin not to kill me too?"

"It's complicated. He realized the money source for this contract kill came through a convoluted channel, from people he despises."

"Are you saying mercenaries have scruples?"

"It involves a matter of love too." Murphy's grin was enigmatic. "I was able to establish a common bond."

"Love?" Aster scoffed. "You *love* me? You don't even know me. And having shared beliefs with a serial killer! This makes no sense. Wait. How does this involve my father?"

"Damn," said Murphy. "It's not fair you can read my thoughts, Aster. I had to swear to him I wouldn't—"

"Screw that! You can't keep secrets from me, Murphy!"

She picked up a bar towel and tossed it in his face. "Go to hell! And thanks for your lack of trust!"

"Aster! Wait."

She walked away, turned, and raised her middle finger.

"I only see *half* of a peace sign."

She ignored his joke and kept walking.

"Please, Aster! Let me explain!"

He sighed, watching as she talked to a customer. She poured wine into two glasses. She deposited cash in the register. The man returned to a table where a woman was waiting for him.

Murphy finished his beer and was about to leave in defeat when Aster walked back. He had to avert his eyes from her stare.

"I can't believe this murderer has any feelings of remorse for the beheading of my mother."

"I know, I know. But he told me, in not so many words, that he has regrets."

"Meaning, he didn't say it."

"I mean, I sensed that he truly does—"

"You *are* a fool."

"No, Aster, I am not. I'm an optimist." He grinned, hoping to raise a smile out from her pessimistic demeanor. "I won't keep secrets from you again, okay? But it's complicated. Trust me."

Aster said nothing, narrowing her eyes.

"So, when should I pick you up for that dinner?"

She huffed. "In another lifetime, Murphy."

12

The atmosphere in the noisy cabin of the helicopter heading toward the Poseidon was chilly. Eldor said nothing as he stared out toward the land and sea. He stroked his beard as he thought with his brow furrowed. Several times Arion prepared a question but was hesitant to open his mouth and ask his brooding father. Eldor turned to scrutinize his son, then he looked away. Arion tensed each time, nearly relieving himself, but was able to restrain his internal organs and maintain bladder control.

The soft helicopter landing did not coincide with the plunge and fall – like a rollercoaster drop – that Arion felt. He was eager to exit the claustrophobic interior, but as he prepared to depart, his father placed an arm across his chest.

"Wait here a moment," said Eldor.

Arion pissed himself a miniscule amount. He could not afford to show any signs of weakness, so he remained still, feeling the seeping urine creep through his underwear. He listened to the rotor blades as they gyrated to a halt, watching as Eldor's henchmen escaped the helicopter.

"I want you to return to that place. The Goddess Bar."

"Why?"

"Because I *said* so." Eldor was annoyed that he was questioned. "You claimed my daughter was evil. I want solid proof. Take Morris with you when you go."

Arion almost asked "Why?" but held his tongue.

"Confront her. Challenge her. See how she reacts. I want Morris as a witness to what transpires. Questions?"

"Confront her specifically. How?"

"She has motive," said Eldor. "This daughter of mine showed

anger toward me for seducing her mother."

No surprise, thought Arion, just like you raped my mother and then abandoned her too. He knew not to verbalize his resentment.

Pausing to rub his unruly beard, Eldor's gaze was moody and unpredictable. He finally added, "She could be the one responsible for these threats."

"The letters?"

"Yes, the letters! She might have connections. It would not be unreasonable for her to want revenge. So I want you to investigate and question her. But be clever about your approach. I sense she is gifted and wily. You are brother and sister, spawn from my blood. I expect her to be formidable. She has her mother's blood too, which worries me somewhat. Ah, but *your* mother was a force of nature as well. That is why I am assigning you to this task."

Arion's non-response, except for a nod, caused his father to react with a stern warning. "Do not fail me. I trust you understand the assignment?"

"Yes, of course, Father."

"Good." With that, Eldor bolted from his seat and departed the aircraft, leaving Arion to follow in his turbulent wake.

Inspecting his pants for signs of wetness, seeing none, Arion stepped down from the helicopter. He felt the eyes of crew workers on deck watching him. Belus, one of his step-brothers, was envious of Arion's status and glared. Belus referred to him as a horse since their mutual father rode him like an animal, and Arion obeyed his every command.

"As if you don't," muttered Arion as he passed Belus, flapping his lips like a horse to taunt him.

Arion returned to his stateroom. He did feel that Eldor treated him like a horse – riding him constantly. His father told him he was destined for greatness. Arion wanted to believe the predictions but his father was a pathological liar. Eldor had several other daughters whom he refused to acknowledge. Why was this newly discovered daughter so special? Because she was the offspring of the notorious Medusa who could kill with one look?

Arion shook off his nerves. He splashed water on his face to refresh himself and wash off the dust from the top of the mountain terrain. He stared into the mirror above the basin. For a split second, he saw the long face of a horse.

Arion shut his eyes and clenched his teeth. When he opened his eyes, the delusion was gone. He breathed deep, then exhaled, telling himself to be fearless. A show of weakness in the eyes of his father was unacceptable. He needed to be as strong as a stallion.

13

Arion took a seat at the bar. His fingers drummed on the edge of the marble top. He took a surreptitious glance toward the back where Morris was stationed at a table, wearing a fake beard and a hoodie. Arion refocused on the wall of bottles.

Suddenly he was facing Aster, looking down at him.

"You again."

"Hi."

"I told you to never come back here."

"That's not being very friendly."

"I can't believe you are my brother."

"Step-brother. One of several."

"What do you want?"

Arion pointed to a bottle. "Tito and soda on the rocks."

Aster didn't move.

"You *do* serve alcohol here, right? Or am I wrong?"

Aster didn't move.

"Gender neutral. No judgement, you said."

"Screw you." She grabbed the bottle of vodka. She scooped ice into a glass, poured the liquor with a splash of soda water, then pushed the drink toward him.

"Impressive." He grinned and sipped the cocktail.

"What do you really want?"

"To get to know you." Arion smiled.

"So, you hate our father too."

Arion choked on the liquor. "Excuse me?"

"It's too early for that. And it wasn't a question."

Aster stared intently at Arion. People at the bar were shouting for her attention, wanting service. She ignored them.

Nate touched her shoulder. "No worries. I'll deal with them."

"Thanks," said Aster, not turning her head.

Arion frowned. "Why so intense?"

She squinted, shaking her head. "That bastard. You, too, are the product of a rape by our father."

Arion squirmed on his seat. "How did you—"

"Know? I don't know." Aster grabbed the bottle of vodka and poured liquor into a shot glass. "So, Demeter was your mother. Goddess of the harvest and sacred law. Which, ironically, includes growing poppies, which produce opium. Is the irony lost on you?"

Arion was baffled by the knowledge this woman, his step-sister, possessed. He self-consciously stroked his facial hair.

"And you work for him. He abducted you into servitude. As he planned to do with me. Except I'm a woman, so he didn't."

"Who told you all this?"

"Only you," said Aster.

"I didn't tell you anything!"

"Your sidekick, Morris over there, doesn't fool me either. But he does fit the profile of a fool. What was your strategy?"

Arion was at a loss, conceding. "To find out if you are evil."

Aster laughed. "Am *I* evil? Don't you see the absurdity behind your words? Our father *poisons* people. And you do his bidding. Who among us is more evil? I only manage a bar."

"You have a point. I could use a refill."

As Aster poured from the bottle, she asked him, "Why do you see yourself as a horse?"

"What?"

"It's in your thoughts. You imagine being a horse. Why?"

Arion drank his vodka and soda. 'You're spooky."

"But not evil." She gulped down a shot of vodka. "It was you who orchestrated the contract to have me killed. Why?"

Arion badly felt the need to pee. "You messed with my mind,

somehow, and humiliated me in public. I am heterosexual. I'm not gay. Did you spike my drink? Because I can't remember how or why I became naked with that person—"

"Shemale, you mean."

"That's not who I am. I would never—"

"You imagined it all."

"What?"

"You heard me." Aster swallowed another shot of vodka. "And your retaliation was to have me killed?"

"Sorry. I will fix this. I—"

"It's already in motion, out of your control," said Aster. "When I realized you were my brother I wanted to like you. But you proved to be a complete asshole."

"I'm not. Really."

"You could have fooled me. No—you didn't. You are."

"Aster. Can we start over? Have a truce?"

She poured herself another shot of vodka and topped off his glass with more liquor. "Do want to see what I can do?"

"I'm sorry, what?"

"Being the offspring of Medusa. Look at me."

Arion looked. He saw her eyes change color from green to a steely grey. He was unable to pull away from them. Transfixed, he watched her hair transform into hissing snakes.

"*Never* mess with me again," voiced Aster.

Arion felt his body stiffen, as if turning into stone. The writhing snakes lunged at his face and he pissed himself.

"Take *that* message home to Daddy." Aster unlocked her gaze from him and moved down the bar.

Still stunned, Arion blinked. He stared down at his soaked pants with urine dripping off the barstool.

14

Arion was haunted by laughter echoing inside his head. He was staring at his father's grim expression. During the silence, Arion's face reddened from shame.

Eldor stroked his beard, then expelled a sour laugh.

"I can't explain what happened."

"You let her win. I told you she would be formidable."

"She's not evil. It's just that …"

Eldor removed a cigar from a humidor box on his massive desk. He inserted it in the hole of a wooden guillotine cutter and chopped off its head. Arion watched as his father bit off the tip of the opposite end, then struck a match, igniting the severed part. He took repeated puffs, exhaling smoke. "What? You don't hate her? Not after what she did to you?"

"I have a bladder condition. She—"

"Humiliated you. In public. You should be furious."

"I am. But—"

"You don't show it."

"It was payback. For insulting her earlier—"

"Morris has spread the story of your ridicule. You've become a joke among the entire ship. Your authority has been destroyed by this woman. By a *woman*. I see no choice but to demote you."

Arion blanched.

"You are no longer the quartermaster. I'm promoting Belus to that position. You will now manage the toilets."

"Toilets?"

"Sanitation Manager. You don't look pleased."

Arion stared in shock at the slight grin within his father's beard and realized he was on Eldor's shit list. His life was in jeopardy.

"Now get out of my office."

Arion rose from his chair, holding his bladder which felt about to burst – like his mind, blown apart. As he exited the Captain's office he saw Belus waiting outside. His step-brother flapped his lips to mimic the whinnying sound of a horse.

"Tough break, toilet boy."

Arion returned to the stateroom no longer assigned to him. He found his belongings stuffed into two duffel bags outside the door and hoisted one over his shoulder. Dragging the other behind him, he went below deck to find lodgings in the cramped crew quarters. On his journey through passageways – passing through a gauntlet of hushed voices, laughter, and a few whistles that sounded like pissing – he felt like shit.

While sitting on his new bed, a makeshift cot, mulling over what had transpired, Arion realized he had to escape for his safety. He sat there brooding until it was past midnight. While his crewmates slept, he sorted through his bags to remove unnecessary items, keeping only a handful of clothing which he stuffed into one bag.

He crept through the ship to reach the lower deck. Stealthily, he lowered the dinghy he had piloted earlier to go ashore. He used the oars to take him a distance away from the ship before starting the engine and motoring toward land.

Arion knew of only one place he could seek refuge.

15

Aster unlocked the front door to The Goddess in the morning, two hours before they opened for business. Once inside, she locked the door behind her and headed toward the bar. She heard a steady knocking. She went back to peer through the glass, surprised to see the face of her step-brother.

Aster opened the door. "What are you doing here?"

"I didn't know where else to go," said Arion, clutching the bag of clothing in his arms. "May I come in?"

"We're not open yet."

"You don't understand. My life is in danger."

"Welcome to my world." She sighed and opened the door wider to allow him to enter.

"Thank you," said Arion.

"Don't thank me yet. I need to know what happened and why you came to me."

Aster locked up again. She walked with him to the bar.

"Have a seat. I'll be on the other side, as usual."

Aster lifted the hinged bartop partition to walk behind the bar, then turned to face him. "It's early, but you look like you could use a drink. Yes?"

"Anything you're willing to offer."

She waved her arm at the array of bottles. I have some chilled Chardonnay in the fridge."

"Perfect."

Aster removed the bottle and pulled down two goblets off the shelf, uncorked the wine and poured. "Demoted, huh? What makes you think Father will kill you?"

"He doesn't tolerate weakness. Pissing in my pants, ridiculed in public, defeated by you, a woman…unacceptable.”

"Toilet duty." She sniffed to show disgust and drank some wine, shaking her head. "Well, you had it coming."

Arion drank some wine. "Is revenge as sweet as they say?"

He lifted his glass in jest.

Aster emitted a laugh and clicked her glass to his. "After what I did to you, I'm surprised you would come to me. Why?"

"It's the last place he would think I'd go."

"Don't count on it. Does he know it was you who arranged for my beheading?"

"No. Can you ever forgive me?"

"I'll think about it. Hungry? Did you want some nuts?"

"Sure. Thanks."

Aster unscrewed the jar and poured nuts into a bowl. "So what now? Do you have a survival plan?"

"I was hoping you'd allow me to stay here."

"You're joking."

"I wish."

"Make another wish. I can't take you in."

He smiled. "But we're family."

"You're unbelievable. Work for me?"

"I'll earn my keep. Is there a back room? A closet? I know you have a bathroom."

"You would work among a roomful of queers?"

"We're all queer here. Right?"

Aster downed her wine. "Let's get you settled in then."

16

Murphy made a return visit to see Perseus at his resort near the sea. It was another sunny afternoon and this Greek and his bevy of friends were lounging in the nude.

"Don't you ever wear clothes?"

Perseus laughed and rose from his poolside station to welcome Murphy, dressed in a swimsuit, shouting, "Rejoice!"

Grasping Murphy by the head, Perseus kissed him on the lips. Murphy didn't know how to respond, taken aback.

"It is an ancient Greek tradition, a sign of respect, Mitch. Do not be shocked by my kiss."

"I'm not. It's fine."

"Come join us. Get naked. Have you grown any bigger?"

"I'm not here to sunbathe or talk about my size."

"No? How sad."

Laughter arose from the crowd of sunbathers.

"Then why *are* you here?"

"Would you like to meet the person who commissioned the beheading of the daughter of Medusa?"

"Do you jest, friend?"

"Not at all," said Murphy. "He wants to meet with you. Do you have anything to wear?"

"Several sarongs. I prefer my chiton."

"What's that?"

"A short tunic. A mini skirt not in fashion these days."

"In the place we'll be going, it won't raise an eyebrow. No one will object to your choice of clothing."

"Then I will don my best chiton. When do we leave?"

"Today. Now?"

"In what mode of transportation?"

"I have a rental car. The destination is a bar along the coastline, not that far from here."

"I am excited to meet this man who hired me and now wants to rescind the kill. Unless he is expecting a refund?"

"No, nothing like that," said Murphy.

"I like this man already. Andromeda needs to come too."

"Why?"

"Have you ever been in love, Mitch?"

"Yes. As I told you."

"Then why do you ask?"

Perseus clapped his hands to alert his wife. "We are going on an adventure, my love! Hurry, we need to get dressed."

"I'll wait for you out front in the car."

"How will I find you?"

"It's a red Jaguar."

"I didn't take you for one so sporty."

Perseus kissed Murphy on the lips and departed.

17

It was late afternoon. The Goddess had only a few customers. Stationed behind the bar, Aster was looking down upon the group of men and one woman taking seats at the end of the bar.

She glowered at Perseus. "You murdered my mother."

"That was a long time ago. And a mistake." Perseus shrugged and lifted his glass of champagne. "What are we celebrating?"

"Nothing," said Aster. "This was Murphy's idea."

Perseus toasted Murphy and drank. "Hum, this is quite good. Apologies, I suppose, are in order. I apologize. There."

Aster was still fuming. She glanced back and forth at the four individuals before her. The man she hired, who claimed to be in love with her; her step-brother, who had a contract kill taken out on her; a women she had yet to meet, who was more beautiful than anyone she had ever seen; and the man who beheaded her mother. It was all so bizarre, so absurd, she laughed.

"Not in my wildest imagination," she said, "did I picture my mother's assassin as one who'd be wearing a skimpy dress."

"It is a *chiton*," said Perseus. "Very traditional and high fashion for its time."

"Since when?" She gulped down champagne. "You don't look to be much older than me. You should be old, if not dead."

Perseus grinned. "I am immortal. Let me introduce you to my wife, Andromeda, more lovely than a sea nymph."

"She is," said Aster. "You are."

Andromeda pressed her lips into a modest smile, and sipped her sparkling wine. "Thanks?"

"My wife is not a talker. She was chained to a rock once."

"By you?"

"No. I was the hero who rescued her."

Aster scoffed. "Tell me why you *are* here. I can read minds but yours is really dense, as thick as a rock."

"Mitch invited me. And I was curious to meet the man who hired me to kill *you*."

"Rescinded," said Arion.

"Acknowledged. But no refunds."

Perseus swirled his glass of champagne before swallowing what was left. "And I am here to apologize to you, daughter of Medusa. For the mistake I made."

"You sure as hell did," said Aster. Out of habit, she refilled his glass and the others. "You're lucky this isn't poisoned."

They all stared at their glasses for a moment, then drank.

She said, "Define your mistake."

Perseus straightened the hem of his chiton at the thighs, crossing his legs, before addressing her steely eyes. "Powerful patrons had led me to believe your mother was a monster with snakes for hair. I was told to beware, because one look from her would turn me into stone. Therefore, with a special sword gifted to me, and a polished shield to guide me, I cautiously snuck into her room while she slept—"

"And cut off her head!"

"Regrettably," said Perseus. "I was mortified to discover I had been tricked. Imagine my astonishment. She did *not* have snakes for hair. Her face was beautiful, except for the blood. Sorry."

"What about all the *lies* you disseminated?"

"Well, yes." Perseus drank some more sparkling wine. "You see, I had a reputation to uphold. And what was done was done, despite my blunder, so I made up stories to bolster my status as a hero. Was that so wrong of me?"

In unison, everyone, but Andromeda, said, "*Yes*."

"I suppose you are right," said Perseus. "Now it is my turn to ask. How and why did you hire me to behead this lovely lady?"

He turned to look down the bar at Arion.

"It was a mistake."

"Gee, you think?" Aster twisted off another cork which made a 'pop.' She filled her empty glass.

Arion continued. "The tricky part was how I managed to funnel the money, in order to elude scrutiny. It was convoluted."

"Our father is a drug lord," said Aster.

"This I know," said Perseus. "A true monster."

"The payment to you was intended to be anonymous."

"It was not difficult to trace the source from where it originated. But since I am a mercenary whore, money is money, and I cannot live on wine alone. I initially did not care until approached by your love interest here, Mitch."

"He's not my lover," said Aster.

"But he loves you. No?" Perseus looked at Murphy, chagrined, then at Aster, impassive. "Anyway, Arion, continue"

"The 'why' I did it?" Arion gulped down the rest of his wine. "Because I discovered I am a flawed man with a fragile ego who was shattered by this woman, my step-sister. She humiliated me. I wanted revenge. I reacted the way our father would have. I do *not* want to become my father. I refuse to be. And I am truly sorry, Aster."

Arion wiped away tears.

"Now *that*," said Aster, "was a genuine heartfelt apology. You could learn something from that, Perseus, who wears a dress."

"*Chiton*. Okay, I apologize again."

"Work on that." Aster raised the bottle. "Who wants more? We should be celebrating something. Except I'm not sure what."

Perseus smiled and offered, "Your life?"

18

The atmosphere inside Eldor's office stateroom was turbulent as he stood again, paced, then plopped back down into his captain's chair. He reached for the box of cigars. "Did you want one?"

Triton shook his head, no.

Belus was in the room too, but not offered one.

Eldor placed the end of a cigar into the guillotine and lopped off its head, then wiggled the decapitated object between his fingers. He was making a point, and smoking was the least of his interest.

"I want Arion found, brought back here, and killed," said Eldor. He narrowed his eyes at Belus. "Understood?"

"With pleasure," said Belus.

Triton cleared his throat. "I was unable to ascertain who sent those letters we both received, Father. But the stolen funds, from my quarterly deposit to you, were embezzled by someone here."

"Arion."

Triton nodded. "No doubt he was planning his escape for some time. He needed money to survive. It computes and makes sense that he is the thief, your traitor."

Eldor grumbled. "I had noticed his suspicious behavior of late. He often appeared nervous."

"He even *pissed* himself in public," said Belus with a grin.

Triton said, "When was this?"

"It's of little importance," said Eldor.

"Our sister literally scared the piss out of him." Belus laughed then shut up when he saw his father scowl.

"Sister?" Triton's interest was piqued, shifting in his seat. "This daughter of Medusa? Her. Our step-sister?"

"The same."

"Belus, be silent," said Eldor.

"I did warn you she was evil, Father. This is more proof—"

"Arion showed weakness. He allowed a woman to play mind games and overpower him. I see no *evil*. Only a weak son who steals from me and needs to be tortured, then eliminated."

"Why are you defending this woman?"

"I am not defending her!"

Triton gave a laugh. "Has she spooked you too?"

"Enough!" Eldor slammed his fist on his desk, crushing his cigar in the process. "She is inconsequential. The matter before us and the reason I summoned you both, is to locate this thief of a son. And to find out who sent those damned letters – and why they were sent – as I demanded of you, Triton. Which you failed to do! Now get the hell out of here and do as you were told. Out!"

19

It was past closing time at The Goddess, the middle of the night. Aster had invited her batch of misfits, who had remained at the bar, to regroup at the house she shared with Nate. They were gathered in the living room, drinking digestifs. Nate's girlfriend, Larisa, woke up from all the commotion.

Persius said, "You are incredibly hospitable for one who – well, do we need to revisit our foibles? – was targeted to be killed by me, hired by your step-brother, whom I just met today. Nice family."

Despite herself, Aster laughed. She thought she might be losing her mind. She raised her glass at this weird assassin. "Thanks for not killing me. My mother would have loved you, and you would have loved her, had you not cut off her head!"

"That's harsh. But true. Sorry about that, once again." Perseus focused his attention on Larisa who walked in yawning, dressed in a robe. "And who are you, lovely creature?"

"Larisa. I'm a heart surgeon. Who are you?"

"Perseus. I am a hero. I kill monsters."

Larisa, confused, looked over at Nate. "What's going on here? Is he serious?"

"I am deadly serious," said Perseus.

"What is that you're wearing?"

"Why is everyone so taken with my chiton?"

Larisa added, "I'm not. It's nothing. I shouldn't be surprised by anything anymore. I love Nate and that's all that matters. I'm going back to bed. Are you coming?"

"In a while." Nate blew her a kiss. "I love you."

"That's sweet. I love Andromeda too." Perseus placed his arm around his wife and kissed her on the lips. "The problem, though, is this world could use more love than war." He directed his gaze on Aster, then Arion. "You lit the match. And the fire has not gone out. I fear that it might become a conflagration."

Aster said, "Exactly what does that mean? Am I still on some hit list? What?"

"No," said Perseus. "But Arion knows."

Aster looked at Arion, "What haven't you told me?"

"I embezzled money from the cartel to pay for the contract to have you killed. Father doesn't know. He will, eventually."

"And then there are the letters we sent," added Murphy.

"What letters?" Aster was becoming increasingly alarmed.

"Before I knew it was your brother who—"

"*Step*-brother," said Aster, glaring at Murphy.

He continued, "Not knowing Arion was the source of the hire, Perseus and I contrived a plan to send a message to instill confusion within the cartel. It might have been a mistake."

Aster slammed her fist on the console table and stood. "Another mistake! God, I'm surrounded by idiots! Sorry, Nate. I didn't mean you. How much danger are we in?"

"Father will want me killed," said Arion. "I don't think—"

"Then *don't* think," said Aster. "You never, *ever*, steal money from a drug cartel and think it's going to end well. And when Eldor, our rapist father – who *is* a monster – discovers you two wrote those letters, you will be looking to die." Aster's anger turned to tears. "Me too, because I *hired* you, Murphy. God damn you!"

20

It was only a matter of time before Eldor's thugs showed up at The Goddess, and Aster planned to be prepared. She lightly pinched Nate twice on his arm to signal trouble. He left to warn Arion, who was working in the back, to stay there and not show his face. Aster had advised her step-brother to shave off his beard. She also loaned him her unisex round purple-tinted sunglasses, which he wore day and night.

"You, again," said Aster, looking up at her step-brother.

Triton stood at the bar, looking down at her from his imposing height. He clutched the shaft of a tall cane with a trident head.

"I'm looking for someone," he told her.

"We're all looking for someone," said Aster, pointing. "And we don't allow weapons inside."

"I won't be here that long."

"And your sidekick, Belus. Seriously, another step-brother?"

"How did you know—"

"She's some kind of freak," said Triton. "Aren't you?"

"Did you want a drink?"

"You *know* I don't. I came here for one thing. To locate Arion, your other step-brother. Have you seen him?"

"Yes, a week or so ago. He pissed himself on that stool. He left with his tail between his legs. Why?"

"He stole money from us. Father is in a rage."

"Our common father is a serial rapist. You must feel proud to be the first bastard in our family."

Triton rammed the end of his shaft onto the wood floor. The bar noise went quiet for a moment. "I am not a bastard! Our father was married to my mother, Amphitrite. She too ruled the sea. You, Aster, are the bastard. And an abomination!"

"What's the problem here?" Nate came to stand next to Aster. He was not as tall as Triton but as muscular. "Are you harassing her, mister? Because—"

"It's okay, Nate. My step-brothers were about to leave. Unless they want to behave and stay for a drink. This is a bar, after all."

"We're leaving," said Triton. "But if Arion comes here—"

"He won't," said Aster. "He despises me. I humiliated him."

Triton hesitated to leave. Her remark furrowed his brow. His face reddened, recalling the first time he approached her, seated at this bar, anonymously. Or so he thought. Until she said his name and identified him as her step-brother and a drug lord. What came next he could not explain. He lifted his mug of beer and tasted shit – saw that it *was* shit – causing him to gag and vomit.

She had an incurious smile, before expressing a face of concern, and asked him if something was wrong with his beer.

His anger turned to stupefaction when he looked at the liquid in his glass – what remained – and saw it was not excrement that he had swallowed. He had only imagined it.

"What did you do?"

"Excuse me?" said Aster.

"To me. The last time I was here. It was *you*, wasn't it?"

"I was here, yes. I remember. From what I recall, you couldn't hold your liquor and threw up on yourself."

Triton narrowed his eyes. "You are evil. Like your mother."

"My mother was *not* evil. She was a smart, beautiful woman who became a monster in the eyes of men like you who feared her power and whose cowardly reaction was to have her killed."

Triton sniffed derisively. "I'll be back."

21

Murphy was seated in his attorney's office.

Adriana had never seen him so despondent. Considering his line of work, investigating unsavory individuals who were cheaters and abusers, Mitch was like a cat that landed on his feet, able to stay upbeat. An inveterate optimist.

"She hates me, Adriana. What do I do now?"

"I warned you. She's dangerous."

"But I love her. And it's all my fault."

"She's mad at circumstances out of her control." Adriana drank from the disposable cup of coffee. "Thanks for bringing coffee. I'm not sure about the donuts."

He removed one, chocolate glazed, from the open box between them on her desk. "I felt the need for something sweet. Give the rest to your staff. I need counseling. Advice. Suggestions?"

"Mitch, you don't listen to me." Adriana cradled the container of coffee in both hands for warmth. "You came here to be consoled and coddled."

Munching on the donut, Murphy gave her remark a moment of thought. "Coddled? Adri, I'm not a baby."

"You only act like one when things don't go your way. And you come to me for solace. It's a pattern. Admit it."

"Okay. Fine." Murphy finished eating the donut and was now licking his fingers.

Adriana stared at the untouched paper napkins, tempted to say something about etiquette, but refrained. "Mitch, how long have we known each other?"

Murphy paused to mentally calculate.

"For almost twenty years," added Adriana.

"Since college. What's your point?"

"We've come to know each other pretty well."

"Again, your point?"

"You're keeping something from me." She sipped her coffee to let the remark sink in. "Something crucial to your situation. It has to do with this woman you are pining over. What is it?"

"Can I trust you?"

She glared back at him.

"Of course I can. Adri, she is like her mother."

Adriana frowned. "The mythical Medusa?"

"It's not a myth, entirely."

"Snakes for hair?"

"Categorically, no. But—"

"What?"

Murphy hesitated, shifting in his seat, rubbing a hand through his hair. "She has strange powers."

"She can read people's thoughts. I know."

"More than that."

"Are you going to tell me?"

"Aster did it to me. And I've seen her do it to others."

"Do what?"

"When you look into her eyes. It's a form of hypnosis."

"Go on." Adriana reached for a donut.

"It's like being temporarily paralyzed. You can't move."

"As if turned into stone?"

"Exactly. Then she plays with your mind. She can make you see things that aren't there."

"Hallucinations."

"Yes."

"What did she make you see?"

"I'm embarrassed to say."

Adriana bit into the jelly-filled donut, tilting her head while she waited. "Oh, for God's sake, Mitch, tell me."

"I was completely naked, sitting on the barstool. She smiled and knew what I was seeing. She was simply playing with me, letting me know what she could do. But I've seen her do worse things to people who offend her."

"Such as?" Adriana used the napkins to wipe her fingers, then reached for her coffee. "Tell me."

"I only know from the shocked expressions of humiliation and fear on the subjects' faces. I watched a man fall off the barstool, then stagger catatonic from the bar. If you didn't know better, you might think it was alcohol-related. Your typical drunk."

"You're sure of this?"

"I'm certain."

"Okay. Now tell me what deal you made with the devil to save her from being assassinated."

22

Triton's frustration was palpable. He expressed his anger non-verbally by punching Belus on his shoulder.

"What was that for?" Belus rubbed his arm.

"How in hell am I supposed to discover who sent those damned letters? There's no way to identify the sender. No postmark. No clues to trace. This is an impossible task and Eldor knows it!"

They entered another shop, an antique store, on the same street as The Goddess Bar. They approached the clerk who was standing behind a counter. Belus held up the screen face on his cell phone. "Have you seen this guy? Take a close look."

The shop owner raised his reading glasses. He scrutinized the image of Arion, and shook his head. "That's a terrible photo. Don't you have a clearer picture? I don't think so. No."

Triton kicked over a trash container as they exited the building. "We're not going to find him around here. He could be anywhere. Halfway across the country by now."

"But he will be found," said Belus.

"Eventually. Eldor won't rest until he is caught."

"Then what?"

Triton displayed his forefingers, snipping the air as if they were scissors. "Father likes his gadgets. Have you noticed how fond he is of that cigar cutter?"

Belus winced, imagining his extremities cut off.

Triton stopped in mid-stride, striking Belus' arm again, turning to walk back in the opposite direction. "I have an idea."

"Where are we going?"

"I'm a genius. Tell me I'm a genius."

"You're a genius. What?"

"I know how to flush out and expose the person responsible for sending those damned letters."

"How?"

"We're going back to that bar."

"Why?"

Triton snickered, increasing his pace. "That bitch thinks she can fuck with me and get away with it. She needs to be taught a lesson. I want her to feel fear and be the one who eats shit this time."

"What are you talking about?"

"Get your cellphone camera ready to shoot."

Triton flung open the door to The Goddess Bar as if transported back into the Wild West, prepared for a duel.

Aster saw him enter and sensed trouble. She finished mixing a Manhattan and set it on a tray for the server. She pretended to ignore him. His trident spear struck the floor, startling her. She turned to face his looming presence, looking down at her from across the bar.

"You came back. Why?"

A flash of light blinded her for a second.

"For that," said Triton.

23

Adriana was left speechless. She reached for another donut not bothering to search for a specific one. Taking a bite, she murmured to herself before addressing Murphy. "Are you insane?"

Murphy shifted in his seat. "I didn't know what else to offer as a bargaining chip. I had to stop him from killing Aster."

"By offering to help him kill someone else! You *have* lost your mind over this woman. You've gone off the rails, Mitch."

"I guess I wasn't thinking clearly   "

"You guess? You *weren't*, clearly. It's not only dangerous and stupid – you're breaking the law! You can't agree to do this."

"I already did. And—"

"It's murder! *Murder*, Mitch."

"Let me speak, Adri. This man we're talking about is a horrible person. A cold-blooded killer. A drug trafficker who poisons—"

"It doesn't matter."

"Don't you think it *should* matter?"

"That he is stopped, arrested, locked in prison – yes. But not to perform vigilante justice by teaming up with an assassin."

Murphy reached to grab another donut but then decided against it. He swallowed the last of his coffee instead. "This person, Perseus, Adri, is very persuasive. I've never known anyone like him. You need to meet him."

"No, I don't." She dropped the half-eaten donut in the trash.

"He *is* weird, but not such a bad guy. He apologized to Aster for killing her mother, regretting his blunder. Which I thought was brave and admirable of him."

"Admirable?"

"He explained how he was deceived."

"Deceived. He decapitated her."

"He only kills monsters. He believed she was a monster. He was mistaken. Tricked by powerful patrons who wished her dead."

Adriana tapped a ballpoint pen on her desktop. "You should hear yourself. I never expected you to be so gullible."

Murphy fidgeted with his empty coffee cup. "There's something else I haven't told you."

Adriana sighed.

"To endear him to Aster, I mentioned her special powers."

"Do you think that was wise?"

"He was intrigued. Enough to want to meet her."

"Not to mention the man who hired him to kill her?"

"Him too. He's one of Aster's step-brothers. She messed with his mind. Embarrassed him in public. It infuriated him. He overreacted, obviously, and regrets what he did."

"Hiring an assassin."

"It was a regrettable mistake."

"I am hearing lots of regrets." Adriana was busy writing on her legal pad. "Can we circle back to the reason why you should not agree to murder a drug lord?"

"I swore to him I'd help. Shouldn't I keep my word?"

Adriana turned her legal pad around and held it up for him to see the word she wrote in large letters: NO!

24

Aster entered The Goddess Bar screaming, clutching flyers in her hand. She directed her outrage at Nate, who had arrived early to prepare their establishment for opening later that morning.

"What the hell is this? Have you seen these?"

Nate held up the same poster. "Hard to miss. They were posted all over town."

"That bastard!"

She slapped down the stack of printouts on the bartop. She had pulled them off poles and walls. Her face was prominently displayed, her hair modified to resemble snakes. They were printed with black ink on antique-looking paper with the words:

WANTED: THE SEVERED HEAD OF THE DAUGHTER OF MEDUSA. $500,000 REWARD. C.O.D.

Nate said, "A prank, maybe?"

"Do you see me laughing? COD – cash on delivery! Triton, who you met, is the one responsible for this!"

"Hey, calm down." Nate came over to give Aster a hug. "I have an idea how we turn this around to our advantage."

"Advantage? It's an advertisement to have me killed!"

Nate grinned. "Only if you view it like that. What I see is a great promotional device. Trust me, Aster. And we still have time to turn lemons into lemonade."

"This isn't a fruit-stand game, Nate. He's deadly serious."

"I have a friend who owes me a favor. He can create a roll of stickers before we open for business."

"Why do we need stickers?"

"Gather up as many posters you can while I'm gone."

"Why?"

Nate held her shoulders. "Do you trust me?"

"You know I do."

When they opened two hours later, the doors, walls, and tables were decorated with these posters, including a gold sticker at the top of each with bold black letters:

THE GODDESS BAR WANTS YOU TOO. JOIN US! –

A FREE SHOT OF WHISKEY WITH EVERY DRINK!

Triton was ecstatic to witness a crowd of people surrounding the entrance to the bar. His clever stunt worked. He imagined Aster defecating from fear as men and women fought to be the first to grab and tear off her head for the reward money.

What he found – once he shoved through the horde crowding the doorway – surprised him. The barroom was packed with people laughing, shouting, cheering, and toasting Aster who was stationed behind the bar.

With Belus in tow, Triton pushed his way to her while holding one of the posters with its golden sticker. He was furious.

Aster greeted him with a sly grin. "Welcome, Big Brother. What would you like? Your drink comes with a free shot of whiskey."

He looked at her bright smile and shiny green eyes and became tongue-tied, incapable of communicating.

"Cat got your tongue? That's all right. Because I know what you are thinking. And you *are* right. You certainly *are* one."

Belus became troubled by Triton's abnormal non-response. He was frozen in place, so Belus spoke for him. "He is what?"

"A genius," said Aster. "I just love the poster. An ingenious idea. He's an advertising *genius*." She snatched the poster out of Triton's extended, motionless hand. "I'm curious. Who illustrated the snakes for my hair and designed this brilliant poster?"

Flustered by the compliment, Belus said, "That was me."

"You have talent, step-brother. I had no idea. Why don't you become a commercial artist instead of a criminal drug peddler?"

25

Perseus was seated in Murphy's office, looking content while he gazed around at the interior space.

"I see you have a small office too."

Murphy was dismissive, "I don't need that much."

"If you say so." Perseus smiled.

Murphy tolerated this incessant ribbing, the sexual innuendos. Perseus was not dressed in his chiton, but wearing a contemporary sports coat and pants.

"So, Mitch, how do you propose we go about disposing of this monster who assaulted you, almost killed my Andromeda, and *has* actually killed people by distributing his poison?"

"That is what I wanted to talk with you about."

"You have my full attention."

Murphy swiveled restlessly in his desk chair. "What if we set an elaborate trap to capture him unaware?"

"I like this so far. Go on." Perseus leaned forward.

"And although we desire to have him killed on the spot—"

"We do."

"We don't."

Perseus sat back in his seat. "We do not?"

"He needs to suffer for his crimes. For the death of others."

"Tortured first. I like that."

"This drug lord is arrogant. Eldor thinks of himself as a god. An untouchable. Imagine the worst kind of torture for him."

Perseus scratched his chin. "Let me think. In the medieval days, I recall a few devices. The Wooden Horse was one. Ah, but what the Persians did to us Greeks using *scaphism*—augh, the worst!"

Murphy was hesitant to ask. "What's that?"

Perseus shuddered. "A form of execution in which the victim is fastened into a hollow boat, force-fed, slathered in milk and honey, and exposed to insects that slowly devour the flesh until death."

Murphy shook his head. "Definitely not."

"It is a complex procedure. And would allow too much time for this captain to be found and rescued. What did you have in mind?"

"We let him live."

Perseus laughed. "You jest."

"An assassination would be too kind for him."

"You lost me."

"Think about it."

Perseus frowned, perplexed. "Mitch, my modus operandi is to kill monsters, not allow them to live."

"Caged. Humiliated. Stripped of all power. And reduced to the craven, abominable creature he will be forced to face each day in the mirror as he rots away in prison. That kind of torture."

Perseus stood and began to pace. He grabbed the sword he had brought with him. He brandished it above his head, causing Murphy to cower. He was uncertain this man's intentions, as he had a hero complex. Perseus lowered the weapon and kissed its blade.

"But, Mitch, I was gifted with a special sword."

26

Belus was walking with Triton toward their power boat docked at the harbor to transport them back to the Poseidon. Triton was sullen, shuffling like some zombie, unwilling to talk. Belus couldn't stand the silence any longer.

"Triton, talk to me."

He glanced at Belus, but said nothing.

"What happened back there?"

"Nothing."

"You froze. You said nothing to her. Something happened."

"Do not say anything to anyone! Not a word. I mean it!"

Belus nodded. "Sure. Nothing happened. Everything is fine."

Triton turned his head, scowling. "This is not over."

Belus noticed Triton's forceful stride was off. He was moving down the sidewalk awkwardly. "Did you..."

"Did I *what*, Belus?"

"Nothing."

They walked onto the dock and stepped onto the sizable dinghy where their pilot was waiting, starting up the engine. Belus observed how Triton settled himself uneasily on a seat inside the canopy. Once Belus was seated too, he could smell it. Triton had shat himself. He was trying to hide the fact.

Belus was amused by his older brother's obvious discomfort and embarrassment. The smell of excrement was undeniable. He mused about this woman, a step-sister he never knew he had until recently, who had outplayed Triton, making him look the fool. What was she all about? Was this Aster, daughter of Medusa, evil, or not?

He was puzzled by her remark, saying he had artistic talent. Was she serious? The poster was supposed to alarm and terrify her. He now felt guilty for taking part in a plot to destroy her. And, yet, he was heartened by her compliment. He was confused by the extent to which he relished her praise. He had to admit she was right about his ambitions. If not for his father – who had abducted him, holding him in servitude to smuggle and sell opiates – he might have pursued a career in art.

As they motored in verbal silence on the bay, under a bridge, out into the ocean, Belus thought about the drawings and caricatures he had created during his free time aboard the Poseidon. These sketches and comical depictions of crew workers he illustrated were received favorably, often with laughter. Nevertheless, they were regarded and dismissed as frivolous endeavors.

He once drew a caricature of his father lounging by the yacht swimming pool in his speedo swimsuit, with his bulging potbelly, his male breasts, and burly beard. It was one of his best drawings. But he was afraid to show it to anyone, fearing Eldor's wrath if he caught wind of it. So he crumpled up the paper and tossed it into the sea.

"What are you smiling about?"

Triton's voice woke Belus out of his daydream. "Nothing. I was just thinking—"

"Stop whatever you're thinking about! None of this is funny. We need to find a way to destroy that woman!"

Belus was about to ask, "Why?" but caught himself from asking since he knew why. Triton had been humiliated by her. By a woman, and Eldor could not know of this defeat.

Belus feared this would not end well for any of them.

27

Eldor was sunbathing by the yacht pool. He had a margarita in hand and was toying with the naked breasts of the young prostitute he had arranged to be onboard with him. She squealed, laughing, as she slapped his hand away. He feared no retributions for his actions, for any of his crimes. To be captured and arrested for being a drug lord was laughable. He was clean. His minions did his dirty work. The drug manufacturing, the trafficking, the money laundering, they were all handled by others, and none of it could be traced to him. He was the head of a serpentine consortium which was so extensive and twisted the authorities couldn't see heads from tails.

The topless prostitute stood and removed the bottom half of her bikini. "I'm hot. Did you want to come in too?"

"Not yet." Eldor chuckled and drank his afternoon cocktail as he watched her dive into the pool. Gazing in admiration at her body, he watched her swim through the water like a mermaid doing the breaststroke. He was becoming aroused but couldn't see the result over the mound of his protruding stomach.

"I need to lose some weight," he muttered, but knew he was too lazy, and an inverterate gourmand, ever to do so. He imagined being a sultan and envisioned having a harem at his disposal.

His reverie was interrupted by bullhorn megaphones.

"We know what you are!"

"This is the floating island of a drug lord!"

"Murderer! Murderer!"

"Millions of innocent people have died from your opiates!"

"Scumbag! Go away! Take your poison with you!"

"What the fuck?" Eldor bolted from his lounge chair and walked over to the railing to see what was going on.

Crew workers had also come over on the lower deck to stare at the flotilla of small boats bobbing in the ocean alongside the ship.

"All of you are criminals!"

"You should be ashamed of yourselves!"

"You don't belong here! All of you belong in hell!"

"Leave now! You are trespassing! Go!"

Eldor's escort date came over dripping wet, her body draped in a beach towel. "What's going on?"

"A bunch of crazies. Protestors who don't know what the hell they're talking about. We are inside international waters. *They* are the ones trespassing. Invading our privacy."

"There he is! The fat pig with the beard!"

"Who's your whore?"

"All of you are whores!"

"We know about your money laundering and tax shelters!"

"You are under federal investigation!"

"Soon you will be indicted for your crimes!"

"Enjoy a life behind bars!"

"Your drug empire is about to sink!"

"*Eldor*, can't you make them go away?"

Clutching the railing, he looked at this woman whose name he had forgotten. Cyra, maybe, or Ira?

"Eldor the kingpin! The narcotrafficker!"

"This is giving me a headache. Do something, Eldor."

"I will, *damn it!*" He pointed to members of his crew on the lower deck and signaled for them to meet with him.

"Are you?"

Eldor looked at the woman. "Am I what?"

"A drug lord?"

He scoffed. "I am businessman. The owner of a pharmaceutical company. I don't *do* illegal drugs."

28

Aster was staring at Arion, studying his face. He had shaved off his beard. "Do you want to live or die?"

"Live, obviously."

"Then let me help you."

"I don't know about this, what you're proposing."

They were in Aster's bathroom, standing, facing each other.

"You have nice features. I know you better than you realize, step-brother. Yes, this should work. I hated that beard. But you are still recognizable."

Arion looked at his face in the mirror. "I know, but—"

"Our father believes you have fifty thousand dollars, money you embezzled, enabling you to escape from him. Am I right?"

"That's accurate."

"You could be anywhere. In another country by now. If that was true. But you are broke. Stuck here. I can't have you hiding in the back room of my bar or being here with me looking the way you do. It puts me and everyone else in danger."

"I see your point. Okay, go ahead. Do it then."

Arion removed the ice packs off his earlobes. "They feel numb. How much is this going to hurt?"

"Don't be a baby." Aster pierced one ear with a sterilized safety pin, then the other. She dabbed each earlobe with alcohol, inserting a temporary plug in each hole. "Now take off your shirt."

"Why?"

"We need to shave your arms. They look too masculine."

"You're enjoying this, aren't you?"

Aster grinned. "A little."

"I am not going to shave my legs."

"That's your decision. I have lots of black tights. They should fit you since we are about the same size. Hold out your arm."

Aster spread shaving cream over his skin, using one of her safety razors to remove the hair. She shaved his other arm and handed him a towel to wipe off the residue. "Now raise your arms."

"Do you think this is actually going to fool anyone?"

"Let's find out. Take a seat at the vanity."

Aster sorted through her assortment of makeup products. She brushed on a primer and added foundation over his skin to conceal any hair follicles. Next, she took tweezers to his eyebrows.

"*Ouch*," said Arion.

"Hold still. I'm making good progress."

Aster plucked away hairs between his eyes, widening the brows and thinning them, creating soft angled arches.

"Close your eyes."

She applied shadow to his eyelids, black eyeliner, and made his lashes thicker. She leaned back to admire her work. "Now your lips. Black cherry red. I'm going for a blonde goth look."

Arion said, "You realize I have black hair."

"Yes, I know. We need one more thing. Don't look yet."

Arion kept his eyes closed and felt Aster fooling with his hair, inserting something onto his head.

"Okay, you can look."

She had placed a white blonde wig on his head. He could hardly believe the transformation. He could pass for a woman.

"We just need to dress you, paint your nails, and teach you a few moves. I have lots of outfits for you. And jewelry to borrow."

"Why are you doing this? Helping me, when it was me—"

"Who tried to have me killed? Because you are turning out to be a good person. Someone I like. A brother I can love."

"Who now looks like a girl."

"No, Arion, a beautiful woman."

29

Triton was already in discomfort, sitting in his own excrement with the bumpy motorboat ride making it worse. He was impatient to reach the ship, wash himself clean, and change his clothing.

He was alarmed at the sight of a makeshift armada of protesters blocking entrance for their boat to dock at the side of the ship where there was a lowered staircase.

"Goddamn-it! What the hell is going on?"

The pilot of their boat throttled down, the engine idling as they surveyed the situation. He threw up his hands to express an impasse, but Triton wasn't having it. He moved outside from the canopy with Belus to listen to the flurry of voices amplified by megaphones.

"This is bullshit! Belus, bring me the flare gun and the bullhorn. Bring it to me! Now!"

Belus did as he was told. He returned, handing the plastic pistol with its emergency flare capsules. Triton loaded the pistol. Next, he grabbed the bullhorn from Belus and pushed down on the trigger.

"Move your boats out of the way! Clear out! Make way for us so that we can dock! Do it! Now!"

This demand had the opposite effect. The flotilla of protesters turned their attention of him, directing their megaphones at his boat to drown out his single voice. The blockade tightened.

Triton shouted to the pilot to move their boat off to the side so as not to be facing the ship. Triton then shot a warning flare over the heads of the protesters. "Move away or you will be sorry!"

When the protesters didn't respond to his demand, Triton fired a flare at the nearest boat. It struck the vessel and caused the people onboard to scramble for safety. He loaded another capsule and fired off a rocket flare at a second boat. This one struck the sailboat's mast and set the mainsail on fire.

Triton laughed, loading a new capsule into the gun. "Take that, you assholes!"

Unbeknownst to Triton, among the small armada was a Coast Guard cutter that sounded alarm blasts. It roared through the other boats toward Triton standing in the idling dinghy.

"Cease fire immediately! Drop your weapon!"

The military crew onboard was armed with assault rifles and machine guns. Triton dropped the flare gun and megaphone.

As the 33-foot law enforcement cutter pulled alongside their boat, two men armed with rifles came aboard, followed by a short stocky woman. She was half the size of Triton but the one in charge.

"Kill the engine!"

After shouting at the pilot, she pointed to the boat's deck.

"Get on your knees! You are both under arrest!"

She pushed Triton who grudgingly obeyed.

"Hands behind your back, big boy. You endangered lives with your reckless actions. You're going to jail."

Snapping handcuffs onto Triton's wrists, she winced.

"*Ugh*. You even smell like shit!"

30

It was late evening. Murphy and Perseus were seated alone at the end of the bar. They were both admiring the wanted poster. In unison, they downed their shots of whiskey with gulps and gasps. They clinked their glasses of beer and drank.

Aster approached them from behind the bar. "What's with the grins? You look like two cats who swallowed canaries."

"Only whiskey and beer," said Murphy.

"What are you celebrating?"

"You, my dear," said Perseus. "Please, join us."

"I'm working. Maybe later, if you're still around."

"Clever poster," said Murphy. "Whose brainchild was this?"

"My nemesis, Triton," said Aster. "He hoped a mob of bounty hunters would decapitate me. His plan was foiled when Nate came up with the idea of adding this promotional sticker."

"Clever bloke." Perseus toasted Nate pouring beer.

Murphy noticed there was a new worker at the bar. "When did you hire her? She's different. Rather fetching."

"She is, isn't she?"

Aster signaled for this person to come over. She wore a grey blouse, black leather skirt, and matching tights. Her bleached-blond hair framed her face with dark makeup and pink-tinted sunglasses.

Aster said, "This is Ari, my new employee."

Ari tilted her head in greeting.

"Nice to meet you. My name is Mitch."

He extended his hand. Ari reached over the bartop to shake his hand with the her fingertips. He held onto her hand, admiring her shiny-black nails, then let go. "Beautiful. I like your style."

Perseus was curious. "You have this familiarity about you. Have we met before?"

"Not in this incarnation," said Ari in a soft voice.

He scrutinized the woman. "I am Perseus. I never forget a face. I will be sure to remember yours." He pointed to Murphy. "We have teamed up to protect your boss from harm."

"Yes, I knew that," said Ari.

"How?" Murphy laughed. "Are you as psychic as Aster?"

Ari's head shook. "I, too, am part of your team."

"Wonderful," said Perseus.

"Welcome to our team," said Murphy.

Aster was smiling. "Still nothing? No clue, Sherlock?"

"What do you mean?"

"Ari, see, you passed the test with flying colors."

"It's me, guys. I need to be unrecognizable."

Perseus heard the masculine voice. He laughed, astonished.

"*Quiet.*" Aster glanced at the other customers talking amongst themselves further down the bar. "You inspired the idea."

"Me? I am flattered," said Perseus.

"Lose the beard. Paint the face. Wear a dress." Arion shrugged. "If you can do it, wear one, so can I."

"It was a *chiton*," said Perseus. "A Greek tunic."

Murphy was entranced by the transformation. He was unable to stop staring. "Arion, you make an exquisite woman."

"Aster made me. She gets the credit."

"And remember," said Aster, from now on you must *always* call him *Ari*. If our enemies find out, they will have him killed."

"Speaking of enemies," said Perseus.

"We have good news," added Murphy. "We orchestrated a coup that went better than planned."

"Your nemesis, Triton, was arrested. He is in jail."

31

Eldor was enraged by the debacle. Triton, his eldest son, who ran half his business operations, was now incarcerated. And Belus, his quartermaster, was locked up too, unable to do his bidding. His pharmaceutical company was already under federal investigation for involvement with drug cartels who trafficked their opioid products. Several doctors had been indicted for prescribing excessive quantities of oxycodone and hydrocodone. Countless deaths from their drugs laced with fentanyl were causing overdoses. Rumors were circulating that Eldor, himself, could be indicted.

Standing outside The Goddess Bar, Eldor screamed into his cell phone, demanding legal action from his attorneys to get both sons released from custody. Morris, and two of his henchmen, were there with him, staring at customers as they entered and left the building. Eldor ended the call with a look of disgust.

Morris asked, "What's the word?"

"No word," said Eldor. "Both are being held. They have to face a judge who will review the charges and set their bail. Nothing can be done until they appear in court."

"When is that?"

"The fuck if I know, Morris. No more questions. Come on."

Eldor led the way into the bar. He searched the room, saw that it was crowded. All the booths were occupied. He walked over to a couple seated in one of them.

"We have a party of four. Find another table."

Intimidated by Eldor's words, not a suggestion but a demand, the man and woman slid from the booth with their drinks in hand, muttering complaints.

One of his henchmen grabbed the man. "What was that?"

"Nothing. We're leaving. Leave us alone."

Eldor slid into the booth with the others following. Once he had settled into the padded vinyl seating, Eldor stared across the room at Aster. She was tending bar and had witnessed the commotion. He kept staring intensely at her as if his eyes were laser beams. His objective was to make her uncomfortable.

No one came to their table to wait on them. Aster gestured to one of the servers, a blonde woman who vehemently shook her head. The other waiters were busy serving customers, so Aster opened the bartop partition and came over herself.

"That was rude behavior and what I expect from you, Father. What is it you want?"

"Alcohol. A round of your IPA on tap. And answers."

"Drinks we offer. Answers are optional."

"Is it coincidence," said Eldor, idly picking up the wanted poster on the table, "and not my imagination, that trouble has followed me since the moment I came into your bar to introduce myself?"

Aster sniffed a laugh. "It began when you raped my mother. No, probably *way* before that incident."

"Question: Are you the one responsible for assembling that rally of protesters who came to the Poseidon, shouting insults and threats through megaphones to harass me?"

"I have no idea what you're talking about. But I'm not surprised there are people who hate you. I, myself, am indifferent."

"Indifferent?" He smiled. "But I gave you life."

"Mother gave me life. You were simply an unfortunate excuse for a sperm donor."

She pointed at her face on the wanted poster. "My severed head? Real amusing, *Dad*. I'm sure you know nothing about this, right? Someone else will be delivering your beers."

32

After being booked, fingerprinted, and photographed holding numbers to his chest for a mugshot, Triton was sullen, squatting on a cold, stainless-steel toilet seat. Belus was sitting on a cot, looking down on Triton as he tried to clean himself. The other inmates in the holding cell were watching too. The humiliation of his debasement was boiling inside him. His underwear was soiled. He pulled up his pants, fastening the buttons. The police had taken away his belt. He washed his hands in the metal sink.

"Who made you shit yourself, Bro?"

"Fuck off," said Triton.

"Bro, you still stink."

Triton grabbed the talker by the shirt and pulled him off his cot. He shoved the man onto the floor and kicked him.

"Do you want to die?"

The man cowered and shook his head.

"Then shut up!"

Triton took possession of the man's empty bunk. He glared at the others in the dimly lit cell before directing his anger inward. It was now evening. The hours passed slowly as he plotted his revenge while the others slept and snored. His step-sister was to blame for his incarceration. None of this would have happened had she not caused him to shit himself. She possessed some kind of strange power. He was convinced she was evil.

Having nodded off, Triton was startled awake by the noise of the cell door sliding open.

"Rise and shine, inmates. Time to wake up and get ready to face the judge. Move it!"

The jailer instructed the five men to vacate the holding cell and walk single file down stark concrete hallways. They passed through the drunk tank, a filthy tiled room with drains to deposit the vomit. They were ushered into a small, windowless room with a flickering ceiling light. The door closed behind them and they sat on a wooden bench. They waited in silence.

Belus, seated next to Triton, muttered, "What next?"

Triton clenched his jaw, saying nothing.

"This is hell," said Belus.

Triton knew it was intentional, the psychological conditioning, how they were led through a maze, now locked in a claustrophobic room with no sense of time or purpose.

A man dressed in a suit and tie ducked through the door and closed it behind him. He held a leather notepad. He sat at the end of the bench and opened the notepad, clicking a pen. He proceeded to read off each of their names, checking them off, and describe in detail their alleged crimes. He identified himself as a defense attorney and asked if any of them needed a court-appointed lawyer.

"I have several attorneys," said Triton. "Where are they?"

"Waiting inside," said the attorney.

A burst of light appeared at the opposite end of the chamber. The opened door was like sunlight beaming into a cave. A uniformed security officer poked his head into their small space and announced Triton's name, summoning him.

The contrast was equivalent to transitioning from night to day. Triton squinted, adjusting to the courtroom's brightness and all the people present and formally dressed. Lacking sleep and unwashed, Triton looked by comparison to be a filthy rat surrounded by clean, watchful cats. He recognized his attorneys who waved him toward a table facing the judge's elevated bench. He was not pleased to see the man who would determine his fate – someone he had stood before on a previous charge. The judge's face expressed a mood as black as his robe once he recognized Triton.

33

It was after closing time at The Goddess. The only ones inside were Aster, Nate, Arion, Murphy, and Perseus, seated in a booth. They were drinking brandy alexanders with kahlua.

"Triton will get released from jail," said Aster, "What you two have done may have made my situation worse. Thoughts?"

Murphy was miffed by her remark. "First, let me remind you, it was your father who came to visit you here. Second, you hired me to investigate who he was and why he came to find you after all these years. Which I accomplished, also resulting in me being hospitalized. And, third, I discovered an assassin had been hired to kill you."

"My fault. Sister, I am really sorry." Arion sipped his drink.

"I've forgiven you," said Aster.

Murphy went on, "So I warned you. I have only tried to protect you, Aster, and stop people from murdering you."

Perseus raised his glass in a toast. "Mitch convinced me not to kill you. His actions were brave. And now we are friends, a united team. That has to count for something."

"It does," said Aster. "Thank you. But what do we do?"

"I propose we cut off the head of that *damned* snake."

His words alarmed her. "Whose head? Mine?"

"*No.*" Perseus laughed. "Your father, Eldor, the opioid kingpin. But Mitch, your ardent lover, advises against it."

Murphy glanced at Aster before turning back to Perseus. "Times have changed. Your special sword, whatever it is, cannot compete with today's arsenal of assault weapons."

"You make a good point."

"We need to figure a way to have him incarcerated."

"Like Triton?" Aster was cynical. "Who will get released on bail and come after me with a vengeance? Great idea."

Nate spoke up softly. "Aster, I hate to say this—"

"Then don't. What about my unique powers?"

"I've been wanting to ask you about those," said Perseus. He looked toward Murphy. "But I was waiting for the right time."

Aster said, "What did you tell him?"

"I had to tell him something. And it worked. He was intrigued and wanted to meet you. And help us."

"This is true, daughter of Medusa." Perseus grinned. "There is no judgement here, you have said. It is a safe haven. So tell us what you can do and how you do it."

Aster let her silence speak for her. These were friends she hoped she could trust. "I don't know. I inherited this gift from my mother. She could mentally manipulate others. Hypnotize with her eyes."

"And turn men into stone?"

"Metaphorically. She was *not* a monster."

"Again, my blunder," said Perseus.

"I can also read minds."

"This we know," said Murphy. "Also spooky."

"And, I can make people see what I want them to see."

"You literally scared the piss out of me," said Arion.

"You had it coming. I find it hard to control my emotions when I confront someone whose intentions I see are bad."

"I warned you. This ability has put you in harm's way."

Aster looked at Nate. "No, you're right. This *is* my fault."

"Not true," said Murphy. "Your father is the one to blame."

"He's tenacious. Maybe that's what I inherited from him."

Murphy kept staring at her step-brother. "Ari, you are stunning to look at. How much effort does it take for you to look like that?"

Aster interjected, "A lot. Being a woman takes work, Murphy. And, for the record, I do appreciate all you have done for me."

34

The judge looked up from his paperwork to look down upon Triton with a sardonic smile.

"Look who has come before me once again. You cannot seem to stay out of trouble. You may rise."

Triton stood to hear the judge read the formal charges against him. This included the use of a deadly weapon, reckless disregard for the lives of others, destroying personal property – a sailboat set on fire – which caused bodily harm and individuals to be hospitalized. Two victims were at a hospital burn center, in critical condition.

"What do you have to say? How do you plead?"

Triton glanced at his attorneys, then said, "Not guilty."

The judge withheld a laugh, shaking his head, staring down at his notes. "Are you aware that videos of your actions were captured on several cellphones? Would you like to reconsider your plea?"

"No," said Triton. "I am innocent."

"Innocent. Until proven guilty?" The judge's smile was spiteful. "Given the seriousness of your alleged crimes, which may lead to a murder charge, plus your criminal record, I am setting bail at one point two billion dollars." He struck his gavel.

A shocked Triton sat as his attorneys abruptly stood to protest. "Your Honor, that is a preposterous amount!"

"Silence!" The judge struck his gavel again.

The other lawyer added, "Your Honor, respectfully, we feel that the bail amount is unprecedented and prejudicial toward our client. Please reconsider. We are prepared to pay a bail bond amount up to one million dollars, a more reasonable—"

"Your client is a flight risk."

"Including conditions that our client be placed under house

arrest and forced to wear an ankle monitor."

The judge stared down at Triton as if considering this counter proposal. He wasn't. Triton sensed it and regretted having laughed at this judge when a jury found him not guilty in his last appearance before him. He had been clearly guilty of his crime, but power and money given to the right people had won his freedom.

"My ruling stands." The judge twirled his gavel by the handle as if taunting Triton. "In these chambers I rule. Your family money and power are worthless here. It will be a jury of your peers – though I suspect there are few people as low and loathsome to be considered your peers – but, nevertheless, they will determine your fate when a trial date has been set. Which could be months, if not years."

The judge slammed his gavel.

"Bailiff, remove this *stench* from my courtroom."

A security officer approached Triton, who was still stunned by the ruling and his loss of freedom. As his wrists were handcuffed, he turned to his two attorneys.

"Do something! Get me the fuck out of here!"

35

Murphy sat on a barstool in front of Arion, watching as he poured beer from a tap.

"Good evening, Gorgeous."

Arion gave him a coy look. "Stop flirting. I'm busy."

"When you get a chance, Ari, tell your boss I have good news."

"Aster could use some good news."

"Why, what happened?"

"Nothing. A minor flare-up. The occasional misfit who disrupts the carefree vibe The Goddess is meant to provide. Nate took care of this drunk." Arion finished pouring two beers. "I'll tell Aster after I deliver these. Did you want anything to drink?"

"My usual." Murphy reached for a handful of nuts. He swiveled on the barstool to take in the colorful environment. He enjoyed the mix of ethnicity, gender, and fashion. His roving eyes stopped on a booth harboring three men who did not appear to fit it. They were talking amongst themselves as they drank from their beers. This was not a jovial bunch. Their expressions were severe and humorless, sending bad vibrations, which Murphy intuited.

"Aster's on her way," said Ari, returning to pour Murphy scotch over ice. "She went in the back room to get a certain wine someone had ordered. What's bothering you?"

"Those three men over there in that booth."

"Holy shit." Ari ducked his head in a reflex. He feared being recognized – even while disguised as a woman.

"Do you know them?"

"Yes. Eldor's henchmen who do his dirty work. Two of them came here before with my father."

"So the question," said Murphy, "is why are they back now?

They don't look like they're having—"

When Murphy turned back, they were gone. "Ari?"

"What?"

"Did you see those men leave?"

"No. They left? Good riddance."

Murphy became suspicious. He had a sick feeling in his stomach and looked around the bar. "Where's Aster?"

"I told you. She went to the wine cellar in the back."

"Who served those men?"

"I think it was Manny. Why?"

Murphy saw Manny at the end of the bar picking up an order. Murphy nearly fell off his barstool to get to his feet.

"Mitch, what's going on?"

Murphy stopped Manny who held a tray of drinks. "Did you serve the three men who were in that booth?"

Manny turned to look. "Son of a bitch. Those bastards ordered our most expensive bottle of wine. And they leave? Fuck them."

"Where's your wine cellar? Show me!"

"After I deliver these—"

"Now, Manny!"

36

Aster finally located the specific bottle of Cabernet Sauvignon. It was listed on their menu but no one had ever asked for it because of the price. Nate liked the idea of including this expensive bottle of wine to make The Goddess appear more classy.

She was struck on the head from behind. She blacked out for a moment, disoriented. She felt her mouth being sealed with duct tape. Next, a cloth sack was placed over her head, blinding her. She was semi-conscious as she fought to resist being dragged across the room, out the back door, and into an alley.

Shoved into the trunk of a car, Aster kicked the inside panel and tried to scream to be heard but it was futile. The trunk slammed shut and sealed her in further darkness. The car bounced on it shocks as people got inside and drove off.

The assault happened fast. Her senses were still groggy, listening to the tires squealing, air hissing through metal, and horns sounding. The vehicle finally stopped. She could smell salt water and heard the sound of boats knocking and clanging against docks.

The trunk opened. She was pulled out. Her wrists had been tied with duct tape. Both her arms were clutched as she was led onto a floating walkway dock. She was guided down steps onto a boat and shoved into a padded seat. She heard an engine start. The boat moved slowly before speeding up, crashing over waves.

Aster flinched as she felt a hand reach inside the sack, touching her face – ripping off the duct tape.

A man's voice told her, "You can scream all you want now. But the sack remains."

"We were told to avoid looking into your eyes."

"I don't buy that paranormal shit but those were our orders."

"I say we cut off her head now before we deliver her."

"What do you say, guys?"

Aster remained silent, listening to the voices of the three men and their laughter. "You are not going to behead me."

"We might, darling."

"Let's have some fun first. I say we rape her!"

"You won't. My father warned you not to harm me."

"How do you know that? Did—"

"This is about Triton."

"No one said anything about—"

"So, he is still behind bars without bail."

"We're not telling you—"

Aster laughed. "It's payback. The judge hates him. It serves him right. It wasn't my fault he got arrested. He has anger issues."

The three men went silent, spooked by their captive.

"Don't worry," said Aster. "I won't harm you. You three are my father's stooges who do his dirty work. I can clearly see that you hate my father too."

"You see nothing. There is a sack over your—"

"Except you fear his wrath. So you do nothing about it."

"Stop talking, missy."

"None of you are my step-brother, thankfully. I have too many of them already."

"I said, shut up."

"You'll never challenge my father because you are all cowards. Even though you have talked about betraying him."

"Enough, *bitch*, or I'll duct-tape your mouth again!"

She laughed. "All of you are afraid of me."

"You don't scare us, you stupid twat."

"Then I dare you to remove this sack off my head."

37

The pilot of the motorboat pulled alongside the towering yacht where a stairway hung from its side. Aster stepped off the boat and onto the ramp. She climbed the stairs to the main deck. She came upon one of the crew working nearby.

"How do I find the Captain? He is expecting me."

The man looked puzzled, wondering how, when, and where she had come from. "And you are?"

"His daughter."

"Come with me."

Aster followed him into the interior of the ship, up a circular staircase, and onto the upper deck. He led her to a closed door.

"You'll find the Captain in there."

Aster knocked and entered before waiting for a reply.

Eldor was behind his desk smoking a cigar, surprised to see her enter his stateroom alone. "Where is—"

"They're indisposed. Taking naps."

Eldor blew out smoke, smiling. "Take a seat. Have a cigar."

"I don't smoke. Put that out. It's ghastly in here."

"This is my personal space and—"

"Why did you have me abducted?" She sat in a chair facing him. "My head still hurts from being hit with a bottle by your goons and tossed into the trunk of a car. I didn't enjoy the ride. Why?"

"You and your friends have been causing trouble."

"I am not the reason Triton is in jail."

"So you *do* know about that. Tell me how—"

"I can read minds. Your henchmen inadvertently told me."

Eldor studied her. "You are like your mother. Aren't you? With some kind of weird powers. Along with your beauty."

"Is that a compliment?"

"That was part of the attraction I had for her."

"Was this before or after you raped her?"

"Daughter of mine, your mother seduced me."

"Liar."

"That would depend on whose version you believe."

Aster gave him a smile, realizing, "You fear me."

"Don't make me laugh." Eldor took a puff from his cigar then ground it out on the top of an ashtray in the shape of a human skull. To refocus on Aster, he brushed away smoke and rubbed his eyes. "If your powers are so strong, why haven't they worked on me?"

"Who says they haven't?"

Eldor frowned, confused by her impish grin.

"Look at the clock," said Aster. "The passage of time."

Eldor realized over an hour had gone by since she entered his cabin. "That is impossible. What is going on?"

"I had ample time to wander about your office. You keep a gun and a knife in your top drawer. Important papers are filed in one side drawer. In the other are articles about the history of your industry. How you went from being a legitimate pharmaceutical company to an opioid trafficking operation, so lucrative that drug cartels wanted to profit from the poison you are peddling."

Eldor huffed. "You operate a bar. Alcohol is also a drug."

"True. But people are dying from your flood of opioids and pills now laced with Fentanyl."

"Our original intent was never—"

"To get in bed with Mexican drug cartels?"

"It's more complicated than you think." Eldor rubbed his eyes. "You had me completely defenseless, whatever you did to me. If you hate me so much, why didn't you kill me when you had the chance?"

"Because I don't kill people, Father. That's what you do."

38

Murphy found the broken bottle of Cabernet Sauvignon on the wine cellar floor, which confirmed what he feared.

Murphy looked at Manny. "Those men kidnapped her."

"Why? What do they want with Aster?"

After looking into the alley and finding nothing there, Murphy called Adriana on his cellphone. She was the one he reached out to when he sought help and counseling.

Nate and Arion arrived in the backroom after they saw Murphy running through the bar into the back room.

"Aster is gone," said Murphy. "Abducted."

"Shit, this is bad," said Arion.

Nate punched the wall. "God damn it! What the hell do we do? Call the police?"

"They won't know how to help us," said Arion.

"It would be a waste of time." Murphy poked his cellphone, holding it to his ear.

"Who are you calling?"

"Perseus."

"Why? He can't do anything!" Nate kicked over an empty beer keg in frustration, causing a racket as it rolled across the floor.

"My father is likely behind this," said Arion.

Manny noticed the change in Arion's voice. "Whose father are you talking about?"

"Mine and Aster's."

"Are you not a woman? You're *not*. You're a man! I *know* you. You once called me a queer!" He laughed. "Look at you now!"

"It's a disguise, Manny."

"My *god*, Ari, you had me completely fooled. You are actually quite attractive as a woman. And appealing to me now."

"Manny, enough!" Nate grabbed his arm and pulled him. "Help me clear everyone out. We need to close the bar."

Murphy and Arion followed them into the main room where Nate raised his voice to announce the bar was closing early due to unprecedented circumstances. All drinks that had not been paid for were on the house.

It took awhile to clear the place. As people were ushered out the door, Adriana arrived, manuevering through the departing crowd.

"What happened, Mitch?"

"Three men abducted Aster. We're not sure what to do."

"Did you call the police?"

"There's no point," said Murphy.

Adriana glanced around the room, saw the wanted posters on the walls, and picked up one off a table. "She could be dead by now if someone took this offer seriously."

"Or maybe they're planning to hold her for ransom?"

Adriana looked at Nate. "Who would they call?"

"They might call here, expecting answers."

"We wait and do nothing?" Murphy said, "That is no plan."

"I recognized those men. They work for my father."

Adriana scrutinized this woman with a deep masculine voice. "Whose father? And who are you?"

"Aster's step-brother. If he is behind this, Aster could be on his ship right now. That's where I would search first. Except I can't be seen. If I'm recognized, my father will have me murdered."

Adriana frowned. "Should I ask why?"

There was a banging at the front door. It was Perseus. He was dressed in his Greek chiton holding his sword.

"I came as fast as I could. Who am I to kill?"

39

Triton's anger and embarrassment made his face turn almost as pink as the jumpsuit he had been issued and forced to wear.

Belus tried not to express shock at his older step-brother's hair and wardrobe. His thick locks, that once flowed off his shoulders, had been cut short. Triton's trademark attire of leather jacket, black denim jeans, and boots, his statement of strength and intimidation, had been confiscated.

Belus didn't know what to say. "How are you doing?"

Triton scowled. "How do you think? That bastard judge has it out for me. I'm a security risk. And long hair is forbidden, I was told, because inmates hide weapons and contraband. *Bullshit*. This pink outfit is their way of mocking me, saying I am no longer in charge. Also to ward off my attempts to escape."

"You don't look that bad. I mean—"

"Fuck you. What the hell are our lawyers doing?"

Belus averted his eyes, noticing an attractive woman who was visiting another inmate. Triton snapped his fingers. Belus returned his eyes to focus on Triton.

"They're tied up in red tape. The judge has denied every motion our attorneys have made – to reduce the bail, to dismiss the case, to suppress evidence. Videos were taken that document your actions. It's not looking good."

"Fuck."

"I heard you waived your rights for a speedy trial. That was probably a smart move."

Triton groused. "My asshole attorneys convinced me I should. They told me they need more time to prepare a defense. They better know what the *fuck* they're doing."

Belus agreed with a nod, even though he felt relief that Triton was locked behind bars. Avoiding direct eye contact, he was hesitant to add, "The prosecution has requested a continuance too."

"Fuck."

"More time to collect evidence from eyewitnesses. Our lawyers didn't object because they need to build a strong defense – to come up with some strategy for you to avoid extensive prison time."

"*Fuck.*" Triton rubbed his mouth, staring at the ceiling.

"You probably don't want to hear this, but the DA is pursuing a stiff sentence. Because of the severe injuries incurred when you set that boat on fire."

"That *bitch* is to blame, god damn it."

"I know, but I overheard them say this could push your trial date back several months. If not a full year."

"Fuck!" Triton slammed his hands onto the metal table.

The officers on guard moved toward him.

Triton raised his arms, a show of surrender. "No problem here. It won't happen again."

Triton lowered his voice, telling Belus. "Get me out of here."

"How?"

"I don't care how. Make it happen. When I get out of here I am going to kill that woman. Has she been captured yet?"

"It's in play. She should be on the ship by now. I instructed our guys to place a bag over her head, as a precaution."

"Daughter of *Medusa*. She needs to die."

"Father warned the men not to harm her. He wants to see her first, before she is locked below deck in the brig. I believe he is saving her for you to play with."

"Good."

Belus nodded, but anticipated nothing good coming from any of this. Never from Triton.

40

More than an hour had passed since Aster had been abducted. Nobody had called The Goddess Bar to ask about the reward money. Adriana was advising they contact the police.

Nate, Murphy, Perseus, Arion, and Manny were conflicted as to the best course of action.

Murphy said, "Once the police see these wanted posters, we will be inundated with questions. If this was a legitimate threat, why did we wait so long to contact them? Those kinds of questions."

Nate said, "My idea of turning these prints into a promotional item might have been a horrible mistake."

"Don't beat yourself up," said Arion. "It was a brilliant idea. This is not your fault."

"We're wasting precious time." Perseus was pacing the floor with his sword. "I propose we charter a boat, find a means to board that vessel, and demand Aster's release."

"And get yourselves *killed* in the process," said Adriana.

"Might the Coast Guard be willing to get involved?"

Nate said, "That's a great idea, Manny. If we explain—"

There was a rapping on the glass of the front door.

"Murphy," said Nate, "Go see who that is."

It was Aster, standing outside. Alone. Murphy opened the door and grabbed her into a hug. "Oh, my God, you're alive!"

"I'm alive." She separated herself from his embrace, kissing him on the cheek. "Thanks for caring."

She was surrounded by the others, anxious for answers.

Nate hugged her too. "Aster, what the hell happened? How did you escape from those men?"

"They gave me a private escort back here."

Arion said, "Were you, or were you not, kidnapped?"

"I was." She moved toward the bar. "I need a drink. Who wants to join me?"

The others followed as Aster walked behind the bar. She poured herself a shot of Tequila, swallowing it in a gulp. Nate went behind the bar to assist in serving them all drinks.

"Whenever you're ready to talk, Aster, tell us what happened. We were all worried, not knowing how to rescue you."

She kissed Nate's cheek. They hugged again.

Aster looked at Arion. "Our father arranged for my abduction and had me brought to his ship."

"I figured as much. Are you all right?"

"Our most expensive wine shattered. A bump to my head and a few bruises. Sure, I'm fine. Considering."

"I don't understand," said Murphy. "What happened?"

"My capture didn't go as planned. Father anticipated a different outcome. I told him how Triton threatened me. And how I retaliated. I transfixed Triton with my powers. I made him shit himself out of fear. This defeat made him go berserk. His reckless rage is what put him behind bars, where he belongs."

"And?"

Aster looked at Arion. "Our father agrees. He distrusts Triton and fears him more than he fears me. I used my special gift to show Eldor, this captain who raped our mothers, that I could immobilize him. I put him in a trance, left him defenseless. He knows I could have killed him but did not, so he decided to release me."

Aster drank down another shot of Tequila.

Murphy asked, "Anything else?"

"I am teaching Father to trust me."

41

Aster was staring at her admirer from across the table.

"Thank you," said Murphy, raising his wine glass, "for agreeing to let me take you out for an evening dinner. Finally."

"This is my first and only date." Aster sipped her wine.

"I am honored."

"Meaning it is not likely to happen again, Murphy."

He laughed. "Call me *Mitch*, at least."

"Mitch, do you know why I avoid calling you that name?"

He smiled, puzzled. "Enlighten me."

"Out of respect."

He frowned. "Respect?"

"It rhymes with a word I dislike. A word I have been called since I was a girl. A word that is disrespectful. And hurts whenever I hear it used."

Comprehending, he smiled. "Call me Murphy."

Aster glanced around the elegant restaurant on concrete piers over the bay with a lovely view of the city lit up at night. "This is nice. You chose well. I'm impressed."

"Thank you for that. I was trying to impress you."

"You have already, by desiring to save my life."

"But I *did* save your life."

"I meant when I was abducted."

"Shall we order an appetizer?"

"Murphy, there is a good reason why I don't date."

"And yet we *are* on a date."

"Stop smiling. I'm serious. Don't think I'm not attracted to you, Murphy. I am. It's not that."

"You're attracted to me?"

"Let's not get ahead of ourselves." Aster picked up the menu to survey the items. "Do you like fried calamari?"

"Order whatever you like, Aster."

"No, it has to be something we both like."

"I like calamari." He raised his arm to signal their waiter. "I'm curious. Were you frightened when those men abducted you?"

"Yes. I was afraid they were going to behead me."

"We all feared that too."

"Once I was in their motorboat I was able to read their thoughts and knew they were ordered by my father not to harm me. What my father had planned for me was another matter."

"Did he give a reason for abducting you like that?"

"My step-brother had lied to him."

"Triton."

"Yes. It was his idea. He blamed me for causing the casualty on the ocean. When a sailboat was caught on fire and destroyed."

"I was there. I witnessed the incident."

"He somehow convinced Father my powers were too dangerous for me to remain alive. Triton said I used my powers to redirect the rocket flares to strike those boats. He claimed I caused the injuries to people on board. Therefore, I should have been arrested. Triton's lies went further. He told Father my powers were increasing, that I was vindictive, and I threatened to murder them both. It was only a matter of time before I did."

"That bastard."

"Father ended up believing me. I had the opportunity to kill him but did not. What followed was an interesting conversation."

"Ah, here comes our waiter. Time to order."

42

Triton sensed something was amiss. Visitations had stopped. He had not heard from his attorneys in weeks. Belus had sworn to Triton that he would make regular visits to keep him updated on his case and family business. Except he had become a no-show.

Confined to his cell – the iron bars, sliding door, cement walls, bunk bed, thin mattress, metal toilet – was testing Triton's ability to remain sane. His cellmate was equally imposing as himself. They rarely spoke to one another to avoid a confrontation. He knew very little about this man, only that he was accused of murdering his wife with a knife during a domestic dispute.

Triton asked permission to make a phone call. His request was granted. He placed a direct call to his father whose cellphone went unanswered. He called Poseidon's main number. He told the worker who answered to get his father on the phone. When told Eldor was unavailable, not onboard the ship, Triton hung up. He called Belus' cellphone and had to leave a voicemail message:

"This is Triton. Call me, goddamn it! Tell our father I need to talk with him. Why is nobody calling or visiting? What the hell is going on? Call me!" He hung up and was returned to his cell.

His cellmate saw his frustration. "Nobody home?"

Forced to share this small space with a man he hardly knew, Triton looked up at his cellmate perched on the top bunk. His slight smile was neither friendly nor aggressive.

Triton shook his head and uttered, "No."

"You've been cut loose, Dude. Happens to us all."

Triton refused to believe it, angered that it might be true.

A few days passed before Triton was informed by a prison guard that he had a phone call.

Triton stood at the wall of phones, picking up the receiver. He was expecting to hear Belus' voice. Instead it was his father's.

"How are you holding up, Son?"

Triton swallowed his anger. "Not great. What the hell is going on? No one has shown up to tell me anything! Besides blowing each other, what are my attorneys doing? It's like they cut me loose!"

"Calm down," said Eldor. "No one has cut you loose, Triton. Your case is complicated because of the judge's prejudicial feelings toward you. Our attorneys are fighting to expedite your trial date. The prosecution is demanding extentions. Our hands are tied."

"Get them untied! I can't stand being locked up in here."

"You should have thought of that before you lost your temper and fired an emergency flare – destroying a sailboat."

"I told you, damn it. That daughter of yours redirected the flare with her weird powers. She is evil and dangerous."

Silence followed. "You did tell me that."

"Has she been captured?"

"She was."

"Good. I can't wait to get my hands on that bitch."

"You should never lie to me."

"What is *that* supposed to mean? I haven't."

Triton was given the signal his time was almost up. "Is there news I should know about before this call ends?"

"One thing," said Eldor. "You will now be on trial for murder. One of the burn victims has died."

Triton felt his body go cold. He hung up the phone. His options for release became impenetrable. He envisioned a life behind barbed-wired walls. Swallowing his pride, he addressed the guard, abiding by the rules concerning prison protocol: "Mr. Correctional Officer, I need to speak with the warden. Excuse me, Sir. I meant to say the Chief Correctional Officer. He will want to hear what I have to tell the District Attorney."

43

Murphy could not keep his eyes off Aster.

"How was your meal?"

"Excellent. You were right. I do need to eat."

"And the wine?"

"Good too." Aster raised her glass and drank. "You have only been nice to me, and I haven't been that nice to you."

Murphy grinned. "This is nice."

"Do not keep saying you love me."

"I said nothing."

"I have a habit of pushing people away." Aster picked up the dessert menu.

"Did you want dessert?"

She placed the card back down. "No. I push people away when I realize their desire is to get to know me better."

"To date you?"

"That too."

"Men."

"Mostly men. I avoid intimacy."

Murphy watched Aster rotate her wine glass by the stem as she talked, avoiding eye contact. "What are you afraid of?"

She looked up. "You."

"Me?" Murphy laughed. "Are you serious?"

"You don't understand."

"Then make me understand, Aster. You have me confused."

She gave Murphy a direct look. "It is not the same. Nate and I have a close relationship. Yes, it is intimate. But platonic."

"Aster, I wasn't asking you to dinner to have sex with you."

"But you will. Eventually. Won't you?"

Murphy poured himself some wine. "Aster. Let me be perfectly honest with you."

"Please."

"You know I find you attractive. And have feelings for you."

"Of love."

"You can read my thoughts. I find that a little scary. But I'm not afraid of you, Aster. I trust you."

"Why?"

"Call it a hunch." He smiled. "It's why I like detective work."

"What do you detect about me?"

"I'm a pretty good observer. I read people too, but not like you. I can't read a person's thoughts. But I have keen intuition. And I see how you are. You are a kind person, except when you're not to those who lack kindness. Am I making any sense?"

"Go on." She sipped her wine.

"You have a mean streak, reserved for those you feel should be taught a lesson. It comes from a deep hurt. A wound inside you that has yet to be healed."

"You can't heal me, Murphy."

"Let me try."

"You will only be disappointed."

"You need to be loved, Aster. Everybody does."

"I *am* loved. By—

"You know what I mean. Romantic love."

"Intimacy, which I avoid."

Murphy looked into her eyes. "Since we are having this intimate conversation. Can I ask, have you ever—"

"Don't go there. That is not a question to ask."

44

Eldor was feeling weightless, bobbing in the shallow end of his swimming pool with four young prostitutes his personal assistant had selected and escorted aboard his yacht. The women were naked. So was Eldor naked, fully aroused, with Viagra working its magic. He puffed on his cigar, watching these water nymphs dance around him. They took turns diving underwater, toying with his body. Eldor closed his eyes and imagined the lips of fish nibbling on his flesh, teasing him with their mouths. Feeling pure ecstasy, he shuddered, relieved these nymphs were not piranhas with sharp teeth.

His sultan/harem fantasy was ruptured by a megaphone:

"Attention all persons aboard the Poseidon! This is the United States Coast Guard! Lower your hydraulic staircase ramp! Prepare to be boarded! Do not attempt to escape! We have a federal warrant for the arrest of an Eldor Sackler!"

Eldor's cigar fell from his mouth into the heated pool. Having been underwater, the four women were slow to comprehend the noise and dire situation when they resurfaced. Eldor had pushed them away. He walked through the water, ascended the pool stairs, and grabbed his robe from the lounge chair. Feeling vulnerable, naked and erect, and uncertain what to do, he crept toward the side of the ship to peek over the railing.

He saw this was not a prank. It appeared to be a legitimate FBI armed vessel with jurisdiction to intervene. Eldor rushed to get to his stateroom to put on clothes. He contemplated if there was time for his helicopter to be ready for launch. He had already heard the ramp lowered and foot traffic coming up the staircase. He feared being arrested wearing only a bath robe.

In panic mode, Eldor's wet feet slipped on the varnished cherry-wood flooring below the stairwell that led to his stateroom. During his scramble to get up, his robe caught on the handrail, impeding his retreat. In his frustration to break free from the iron nosing, Eldor discarded the robe, and ran naked up the stairs.

He was stopped by a uniformed guard on the landing who held a semi-automatic rifle.

"Stand down!"

A stunned Eldor said, "Allow me to get dressed first."

"There will be time for that later. On your knees!"

The armed man held his gun on Eldor, who obeyed, dropping to the floor. They were joined by a female officer in uniform whose first response was to laugh.

"What have we here? Normally, I would require you show some identification. But you have none to show me. Except the obvious identifying exposé, defining you as male. Are you Eldor Sackler?"

He nodded.

"You have been indicted by a grand jury for your involvement with drug cartels, including money laundering. You are hereby under arrest. You have the right to remain silent. Anything you say can and will be used against you in a court of law. You have the right to an attorney. If you cannot afford a lawyer, one will be provided for you. Now, place your hands behind your back."

"Listen," said Eldor, "I need to get dressed."

She kicked his feet apart. "What you *need* to do, Mr. Sackler, is to obey my commands." She locked handcuffs on his wrists. She grabbed his elbow and lifted. "Stand up."

"Please," said Eldor, "This is highly embarrassing."

The woman smiled, looking him over. "I am not in the least bit embarrassed. But I can see why *you* are. For one purported to be so imposing and formidable, you appear to me as one who is not such a bigwig kingpin after all."

45

Time passed as it always does for the living. Aster and Nate were hosting a party. It was Aster's birthday. At their shared house were Larisa, Murphy, Arion, Ariana, Perseus, and Andromeda.

"What a strange world," said Arion. "I propose a toast to the co-owner of The Goddess Bar, my step-sister, who risked her life to protect me from being killed when I did not deserve her help after what I did. Aster, my birthday wish for you is to have a long and happy life, free from fear."

"Thank you, Ari," said Aster. "I think you, too, are safe now. You can stop masquerading as a woman."

"Except I've grown fond of my new incarnation."

"Me too." Perseus winked at him, then kissed Andromeda.

Arion looked at himself in the mirror to check his makeup and brush a strand of blond hair off his face. "Have I gone mad?"

"No, Ari," said Larisa. "You are very pretty."

"We are all in agreement." Perseus raised his wine glass. His other hand clutched the handle of his sword held upright by his side. He and his wife were dressed in chitons. "I too propose a toast: to keeping our heads while others around us are losing theirs. Ha!"

Aster told Arion, "I feel I've gone mad too. Why did I tell our father I would visit him in prison? I'm conflicted. Should I?"

"Maybe I'll go with you, dressed as I am."

Ariana laughed, "I wouldn't recommend that. Eldor still has powerful connections outside of prison."

"I wasn't serious," said Arion, "only curious to see if I could go undetected as his son who stole his money."

Murphy said to Ariana, "I would never have suspected Triton to turn state's evidence, flipping loyalties against his father."

Ariana looked at Aster. "Your father miscalculated from hubris. For disclosing information about their organization to indict Eldor and testifying against him, Triton received a reduction in his criminal charges and prison sentence. This happens all the time."

"Cowards have no loyalty." Perseus toyed with the sword now held between his splayed legs. "I wanted to kill those two monsters. But Murphy, you were right, a life behind bars is torture, worse than an assassination. Death is getting off easy."

Aster said to Arion, "Eldor raped our mothers. He's responsible for the deaths of many. He abducted you and others into servitude. Now I agree to visit him in prison? Why? I must be crazy."

"You are *not* crazy," said Murphy. "You have a kind heart."

"Speaking of hearts," said Nate. "Congratulate my love, Larisa, for another successful heart surgery. She saves lives too."

Everyone toasted Larisa. Nate embraced her with a kiss.

Perseus announced, "Aster, I have a confession to make."

"Good God, what now?"

"I did *not* kill your mother. My father did. I only inherited his special sword. Before he died, he confessed to me what I told you. He had been deceived. He regretted his bloody exploit. That is God's truth. I am not a hero. I simply rescued my wife from shark-infested waters when she was chained to a rock. I have killed no monsters. But I will someday. There. Honesty. Am I still loved?"

Andromeda turned her head, kissing him. "I love you."

Murphy and Aster were seated next to each other on the couch. He raised his glass of wine. "I, too, propose a toast."

He turned his head to face Aster. "I have never met anyone more beautiful, more enchanting, more assertive, more brave, and more *dangerous* that this woman before me. Happy birthday, Aster!"

They all laughed, raising glasses and toasting assents. Murphy leaned over and kissed her cheek.

Surprised by this unexpected advance, Aster turned and looked directly into Murphy's eyes.

"You know what I could do to you right now if I wanted."

"I know. I'm not afraid."

He leaned forward and kissed her on the lips.

Embarrassed, Aster said, "Why did you do that?"

"I want you. I love you."

"You don't really know me. You may not like what you find."

"I already know. Nate confided in me."

"And you want me anyway?"

"Any *way*, Aster. Yes."

EPILOGUE

There are variations of this Greek myth. The best-known story told about my mother, Medusa, comes from the Roman poet Ovid. According to his poem, Mother was a lovely maiden and a priestess to Athena, the goddess of war and wisdom. She was the only virgin goddess and demanded her subservient, my mother, to remain chaste and celibate for life.

My mother's beauty and lustrous hair made Athena jealous and enraged that her priestess was more beautiful than herself, born a goddess. Athena's uncle, Poseidon, god of the sea, desired Medusa, but she rejected his advances. This only emboldened Poseidon who, typical of a god, took what he wanted and raped my mother in the goddess' temple. She was victimized again when Athena accused her of seducing him – since lovers of a god were elevated as life partners. Athena savagely punished Medusa for breaking her vow of celibacy. The goddess transformed her into a monster whose wonderous hair became venomous snakes. So goes the story.

To make sure no man would want my mother, Athena cursed her with eyes and hair that, with one look, turned men into stone. She was banished to a rocky island. Considered dangerous, people wanted her destroyed. Perseus, a demigod, was sent on a hero quest to kill her. Athena gifted Perseus with her polished shield to view Mother's reflection and avoid becoming petrified. An unbreakable sword was given to Perseus by Hermes, which he used to behead my mother while she slept. It was rumored that upon her decapitation two children – a winged horse, Pegasus, and Chrysaor, a giant boar – flew out from her bloody neck!

None of these tales are factual, only distortions of the truth, except for her eventual beheading. Only I, Aster, a son who became a daughter, was born to Medusa. Once impregnated by this sea god, she gave birth to me. This happened long before her beheading. To hell with all these lies – spawned from jealousy and hatred.

This myth of Medusa gave my mother a reputation for being a wicked woman who turned the living into stone. Like most women of ancient mythology, as well as today, my mother became a victim of patriarchal societal norms. She was an apotropaic woman – gifted with protective magic to ward off harm and malevolent people. She showed courage and resiliency in the face of adversity. The name Medusa represents the personification of powerful women viewed as dangerous, specifically by men who fear female power.

Since I inherited my mother's eyes and was born into a male-to-female body – viewed as an abomination by society – I, too, am a monster. But am I truly? Like my mother, I proudly advocate love and diversity, believing good will prevail over evil.

Am I the harbinger of truth? No, I am a fictionalized character, marginalized, who hopes the living will finally evolve into a world that embraces an open-hearted inclusive anthem of "Yes."

Printed in the USA
CPSIA information can be obtained
at www.ICGtesting.com
LVHW020840260524
781396LV00004B/123

9 798988 275725